Sabine Baring-Gould

Village Conferences on the Creed

Sabine Baring-Gould

Village Conferences on the Creed

ISBN/EAN: 9783742817884

Manufactured in Europe, USA, Canada, Australia, Japa

Cover: Foto ©Andreas Hilbeck / pixelio.de

Manufactured and distributed by brebook publishing software
(www.brebook.com)

Sabine Baring-Gould

Village Conferences on the Creed

VILLAGE CONFERENCES

ON

THE CREED.

BY THE

REV. S. BARING-GOULD, M.A.,

RECTOR OF EAST MERSEA,

AUTHOR OF "ORIGIN AND DEVELOPMENT OF RELIGIOUS BELIEF," "CURIOUS
MYTHS OF THE MIDDLE AGES," "LIVES OF THE SAINTS," ETC.

LONDON :

JOSEPH MASTERS, 78, NEW BOND STREET.

MDCCCLXXIII.

LONDON :
J. MASTERS AND SON, PRINTERS,
ALBION BUILDINGS, BARTHOLOMEW CLOSE, E.C.

PREFACE.

THE importance of instructing the people in doctrine has been too much overlooked by the clergy, who have hitherto directed their efforts to the enforcement of morality. But morality without dogma is a house without a foundation, a flower without a root. The consequence is that our poor have the vaguest apprehension of the great truths of Christianity. Our teaching has been deficient in definiteness. The importance of clear, definite teaching cannot be overrated.

It is a frequent subject of complaint that constant appeals to the conscience tend to blunt it, that after awhile folks like to have their consciences tickled by stimulating sermons, as cats like having their backs scratched. The reason is that we have made our sermons into appeals to the feelings, and have left on one side appeals to the understanding. Let us restore dogmatic instruction to its proper place, and then moral appeals will be more likely to meet with some response.

Lent and Advent are the proper seasons for stimulating sermons, moral and dogmatic instruction may well occupy the preacher through the rest of the year.

The following plain "Conferences,"—to use a French word,—on the Creed were delivered on Sunday afternoons in Trinity season, to a congregation of farm labourers and boatmen. This will account for a local colour and familiarity of illustration which might awake a smile in a more educated congregation. If we want to fertilize the understandings of our people, we must use homely illustrations.

It must not be supposed that these Discourses exhaust the subject of the Creed. I have taken up only one or two aspects of each great verity.

Nor is the teaching as full as some might desire; but it is with milk that our people must be fed before they can digest meat.

Perhaps portions of some of these Sermons may be beyond the comprehension of all the poor in a village congregation, but there are few congregations which do not contain some more intelligent men than the rest, and to them there is little, if anything, in these Conferences which they would not be able to follow. For the rest there is simple matter.

CONTENTS.

VILLAGE CONFERENCES ON THE CREED.

I.

A RIGHT FAITH.

" Let us hold fast the profession of our faith without wavering."—
Heb. x. 23.

YOU sometimes hear it said, It doesn't matter what we
believe, so long as we lead decent lives. But it does
matter, a great deal: for GOD expects of us to believe
aright just as He expects us to act aright. If He has given
us the talent of faith, and has also revealed to us His certain truth, of course He will call us to account for the use
we have made of that talent, and we shall have to show
cause why we have not believed all revealed truth.

He has given us the faculty of believing, like eyes, and
He has given us the truth, like the light of day; and if we
go through life with our eyes shut, or spend our days in a
cellar and only come out at night, we must be able to
account for this, and say why we did not open our eyes,
or why we did not see all the beautiful things of GOD's

B

earth by the clear light of day. Now we have got the power to see divine truth, that power is faith. And God has revealed divine truth to us, so that we are to blame if we do not believe, or if we believe wrongly.

In the next place, we are under actual obligation to believe certain things. At our Baptism we made a compact with God. He agreed to give us certain things, if we would do and believe certain things,—if we would do His will, and believe His truth. We are hired to Him for a wage, and if we do not fulfil, or try to fulfil what we have promised, He is released from obligation to fulfil His part of the agreement.

If a farmer hires one of you to attend to his horses, he expects you to look after the horses, and he will be extremely surprised if he find you, one fine day, hoeing turnips, and neglecting the stable. "My man," he will say, "what are you about here?" "Please, sir, I am tired of minding the horses, and so I thought I would take a turn at the turnips."

Or suppose a mistress has a cook, a housemaid and a nurse. Each has her proper sphere, each her set work. But one fine day she finds the cook in the nursery, she is tired of baking and boiling, and wants to wash and dress the children—there is no dinner that day. On another occasion the housemaid has a fancy to try her hand at cooking, the bedrooms are not swept nor the beds made that day. On a third occasion the nurse takes a fancy for doing housemaid's work, and the children remain unwashed and undressed.

What will the mistress say to cook, and housemaid, and nurse? "I engaged you, cook, to bake and boil. I engaged you, housemaid, to attend to the bedrooms. I engaged you, nurse, to look after the children. You took my situations knowing what was expected of you respectively, and that you could only earn your wage by doing that."

At our Baptism we hired ourselves as servants to GOD, and He sets us our work, to do His will and to believe His truth. If we neglect to believe, or only believe just as much as suits our fancies, we shall certainly be to blame, and shall be called to task for it at the last Day.

You know how that we keep all sorts of time in the island, and the watches differ by as much as half-an-hour. I know that when the clerk comes for the church keys on Sunday morning, I generally ascertain from him what time it is by his watch, and I find that it differs widely from mine. I have got five watches and clocks in the Rectory, and they all tell different times.

But supposing that Mr. R—— were to give us a clock for the church-tower, an excellently made one by the very best clock-manufacturer in London, which he guaranteed to be perfectly correct in its time-keeping,—then we should all have a standard by which we could set our watches and clocks. And when we had that standard the farmers would not take your excuses for being late at work in the morning, and leaving off before your time for dinner, and being away an hour and a quarter instead of an hour, or forty minutes instead of thirty.

No use for one of you to say, as you came sauntering up to your work at half-past seven, when you ought to have been at it at half-past six, "I set my watch by the Brightlingsea train, which one generally hears, when the wind is in the right quarter, rushing over the bridge at noon."

The farmer would say, "Look at the church clock, that is

the standard, not the Brightlingsea train." No use for another to leave off work at eleven instead of twelve, and give as his excuse, " I always feel hungry for my dinner precisely at twelve ; and as I felt very hungry, I knew it must be noon."

The farmer would say, " Look at the church clock, that is the standard, not your appetite." Before CHRIST came and declared the truth to the world, men were like us Mersea islanders without a church clock. Every man set his faith according to some fancy of his own, or guessed what was right by the faith of his neighbours. But when CHRIST came into the world, He set up a standard of Truth, to which He expects all Christian men to look and by which to regulate their faith.

It won't do for you to say, " I set my faith by Mr. Spurgeon," or " I set my faith by John Wesley," or " I set my faith on Independent principles," for GOD has set up His Standard of Truth ; you must regulate your belief by that and not by Spurgeon, or Wesley, or on Independent principles. For if Spurgeon and Wesley have regulated their faith apart from the Standard of Truth, then they are as far out as the men who set their watches, one by Brightlingsea train, the other by his stomach.

And there is something more to be said about having a right faith. We cannot have a right practice without a right faith.

I do not mean to say that there are not good heathens. They act up to the light given to them. It is not much light, but they make use of it such as it is. They are like men carpentering by starlight. They turn out clumsy pieces of work, but still it is the best they can do under the circumstances. They cannot see to make the joints fit very nicely, and make the corners very exact, and to plane the wood very smooth. So the heathen may have a rough goodness, honesty, modesty, piety, and so on; and his is as good a life as you can expect of a heathen.

Nor do I mean, for one moment, to deny that there are good Christians who are not Churchmen. They act up to the light given to them. It is not the full blaze of GOD's truth, but it is a sort of twilight; and if there are, as there certainly are, some far better dissenters than are some Churchmen, the more it is to their credit. They are like carpenters making a piece of furniture in the grey dusk. It is not very perfectly put together, but you do not expect more, they cannot see to make it perfect. But such carpenters are infinitely to be commended to such lazy fellows as do their work badly in the full light of a sunny day.

Now in the Church we have the full blaze of all GOD's truth, but in the other bodies of Christians there is only a little light. If a dissenter leads a good life with the glimmer given to him, he is sure to be rewarded by GOD much more than the lazy Churchman, who with the full faith is content to scamp his work, and lead only a moderately good life. The dissenter is acting up to his full light, the Churchman is not acting up to his.

But if the good heathen became a dissenting Christian, he would become an infinitely better man ; and if the good dissenter becomes a consistent Churchman he advances immeasurably higher in his Christian life.

And this stands to reason, when we consider what GOD's truth is. GOD's revelation contains a number of truths, and not one of those truths is without great importance to us in our growth in holiness. If we do not believe the whole of the revelation of GOD we are stinted in some of the elements of growth. Children, and indeed men, get on well if given bread and milk and meat and vegetables. If they are kept to milk alone they grow very fat, but do not get the muscle and strength they would derive from bread and meat and vegetables. So if we were kept on vegetables without meat, we should lack vigour of constitution ; and sailors who cannot get vegetables are sorely troubled with the scurvy. So is it with our faith. All the articles of God's truth are so many different articles of consumption necessary for the growth and health of our spiritual nature. If we go without some, we are liable to become deficient in vigour of spiritual constitution. If we go without others, we are liable to be afflicted with a sort of spiritual scurvy. And this accounts for what you must have remarked in many good people, who profess to be Christians, and yet who are not right in their lives altogether ; they are selfish, or mean, or underhanded in their money transactions. This is a sort of spiritual scurvy, and is a token that there is one article of God's truth they do not mark, learn, and inwardly digest.

Now lastly. If it be so important for us to hold the right truth, if we shall be required by God to hold it, if we are morally responsible for holding it, having by solemn covenant engaged to believe it, what and where is that Truth ?

The Truth is found in the Creed.

The Creed is like the clock set in the church, whereby we are to regulate our private faith, and when our faith is so regulated, thereby we must regulate our work. It is of the Creed that I am now about to speak to you, in a series of sermons ; but before I begin on the truths we are called upon to believe, I have thought fit to show you how important it is for us Christians to have a right faith.

II.

GOD.

" Hear, O Israel : The Lord our God is one Lord."—Deut. vi. 4.

I DO not myself think that it is possible to prove to any one that there is a GOD. All mankind is agreed that there must be a GOD. It is only the very lowest and most degraded of savages who have no ideas about a GOD. I do not think it at all probable that all mankind should be mistaken in this matter ; and I think it is not for us to prove that there is a GOD, but it is for infidels to prove to us that there is not a GOD ;—and that is an impossible thing for them to do.

If there be no GOD, how did men get the idea into their heads that there is one ? People cannot imagine and be-lieve in something that does not exist. You will answer me, people believed once in dragons, but we know that there are no such things. No, there are no such things now, but there must have been some things very much like them at one time, for we find their fossil bones. Well, you will say, people believed once in hobgoblins ; now we know there are no such things. I beg your pardon. There are such things as devils. Now people do not always believe quite right about things, but I do not think people generally can have had any strong belief, without there being some true ground for this belief. A short-sighted man like myself may see something in the distance and think it a horse, whereas it may be a shrub, or mistake a man for a post. But though he make a mistake about what the thing is that he sees, he does see a something, or he could not make a mistake about what it is.

So is it with faith. Superstition is only short-sighted faith. People see something that really exists, but their faith being short-sighted, they make a mistake about what it is.

The fact of the existence of superstitious and erroneous beliefs in GOD, is an evidence that there is a GOD about whom people make mistakes.

Christianity has drawn a film from our eyes, and now we see, and know, what GOD is. But heathen people and some very clever philosophers have got a veil over their eyes, and so they make strange blunders about that GOD whom they dimly see. As to some philosophers, they have used their eyes so much on little mites of creatures, and atoms, that they have shortened their sight, till they can see nothing but what is just under their noses, and these can scarcely see GOD at all.

So I think that the fact of all nations agreeing to recognize the existence of a GOD is pretty strong presumptive evidence that there is a GOD.

Then again, look at creation. It is easy enough to believe that GOD made the world and the stars and the sun and the moon. How they came into being without a GOD is much harder to imagine.

A very profound philosopher was once arguing that the world was developed out of eternal matter; and that things came gradually into existence. A little child listened attentively, and when he paused asked, " Please, sir, which came first, the hen that laid the egg, or the egg that produced the hen?" That was a puzzler. He could not answer it.

Now, I will tell you another story.

A clergyman once had a friend who did not believe that there was a GOD who made the world, and who ruled the world. The priest, one day when his friend was likely to call, brought a very beautiful globe and put it on his table. It was a peculiarly fine one, and his friend had never seen it. Presently there was a tap at the door, and the unbeliever walked in. He started with surprise when he saw the globe, hastened to it, turned it round, and admired it greatly. "Whose is this magnificent globe?" asked the visitor, "Is it yours?"

"No," said the priest, composedly, "it belongs to no one."

"What a beauty it is. How came it here?"

"It came of itself," said the priest, gravely.

"Nonsense, man," exclaimed the unbeliever, "what are you saying? Do you know who was the maker of this globe?"

"No one made it," said the priest without moving a muscle.

"How can you talk such nonsense! Do you think I am a fool?"

The clergyman jumped up, caught his friend by the arm, brought him to the window, pointed out. Before him was a pretty garden full of flowers, beyond—trees and hills, and far away the sun sinking behind gold and scarlet clouds. "Is not the world lovely, perfect!" exclaimed he; "that globe is only a mean miniature of this vast world. How can I talk such nonsense as assert that this papier-maché globe belongs to no one, came of itself, was made by no one? You think me a fool to say this. Oh, friend, how then can you assert the same thing of this world?"

It really is almost impossible to believe that this world, sun and moon and stars, could have come into being all of themselves, that it could have chanced any how that we have two legs instead of one, that we have eyes at all. Just look at a little new-born baby; perfect in all its parts, the tiny fingers, the beautiful diminutive joints of the fingers, the small nails;—all there, all perfect; and think, "Is it possible that this is the result of chance?"

There is a theory you will hear of in newspapers, which is very fashionable now among those who think the history of the creation of Adam and Eve an old wives' tale. They say that the human race is derived from apes. Let these profound thinkers who tell us we have all sprung from apes, speak for themselves; we prefer to believe that we sprang from Adam and Eve, as the Bible tells us.

It is necessary to speak to you of all these theories of getting rid of GOD and Bible truth, for in these days of reading, and penny papers, and halfpenny Echos, of all the trash and evil that is talked and done, you are sure to hear something of the sort.

Now I will tell you something which I think must be a puzzler to those who hold the theory of developement, as they call it;—which means that we are derived from the ape, and the ape from some other animal, and so back to some fish, and the fish back to an oyster, and the oyster back to a jelly fish. Well, If the type is always perfecting upwards till it reaches its highest perfection in man, how is it that human babies are more helpless, weak and dependent on father and mother, than are the little ones of oysters and jelly fish? The higher the stage of perfection in the animal, the more dependent and helpless the infant, till we reach man, whose babe is the most helpless creature imaginable.

Now I said, at the beginning of my sermon, that I do not believe we can prove the existence of GOD to any man's satisfaction. For GOD is felt, not proved, believed in, rather than demonstrated. The wisest man cannot prove convincingly that there is a GOD, but the merest child can believe in GOD. It comes as naturally to a child to believe in GOD as to learn to walk. It is not easy to believe in impossibilities; and I think the readiness with which we believe in GOD, the natural way in which belief in Him fits in with our ideas, is a very good evidence that our hearts were made to believe in Him.

Heathens have had strange ideas of GOD, and what His nature was, what was His will, how He was to be served. But JESUS CHRIST has brought the truth to us. He has declared to us what the nature of GOD is, what is His will, and how He is to be served; so that we are quite without excuse if we fall into error on this point.

Now this is what we Christians believe about GOD.

We believe that He is a Spirit. We believe that He is everywhere present. David said, "Whither shall I go from Thy Spirit, or whither shall I go from Thy presence? If I climb up into heaven, Thou art there: if I go down to hell, Thou art there also. If I take the wings of the morning, and remain in the uttermost parts of the sea; even there also shall Thy hand lead me: and Thy right hand shall hold me." (Ps. cxxxix. 7—10.)

He is infinitely *wise*. He knows the past, the present, and the future. He can read our most secret thoughts. He that saith, "I am compassed about with darkness, the walls cover me, and nobody seeth me; what need have I

to fear? Such a man . . . knoweth not that the eyes of
the LORD are ten thousand times brighter than the sun,
beholding all the ways of men, and considering the most
secret parts. He knew all things ere ever they were created;
so also after they were perfected He looked upon them all."
(Ecclus. xxiii. 18—20.) "The works of all flesh are before
Him, and nothing can be hid from His eyes. He seeth
from everlasting to everlasting." (Ecclus. xxxix. 19, 20.)

GOD is infinitely *holy*, so He loves what is good and
abhors iniquity. "Thou art of purer eyes than to behold
evil, and canst not look on iniquity," says the prophet.
(Hab. i. 13.)

GOD is infinitely *just*. S. Paul says, "Thou, after thy
hardness and impenitent heart treasurest up unto thyself
wrath against the day of wrath and revelation of the righte-
ous judgment of GOD; who will render to every man according to his deeds." (Rom. ii. 5, 6.)

GOD is also infinitely *powerful*. That is, He is Almighty.
"O LORD, LORD, the King Almighty,"—this was the prayer
of Mordecai; (Esther xiii. 9—11;) "for the whole world is
in Thy power . . . there is no man that can gainsay Thee,
for Thou hast made heaven and earth, and all the wondrous
things under the heavens. Thou art LORD of all things, and
there is no man that can resist Thee, which art the LORD."

He is infinitely *merciful*, and therefore our fears raised by
a sense of His strict justice and power, are tempered by a
consciousness of His mercy. "The LORD is gracious and
merciful," says David; "long-suffering, and of great goodness. The LORD is loving unto every man; His mercy is
over all His works." (Ps. cxlv. 8, 9.) In His mercy He
has made to us great and glorious promises, which are sure
to be fulfilled, for—

He is infinitely *true.* "I am the Way, the Truth, and the Life." "The LORD," says the Prophet Jeremiah, "is the GOD of Truth." (Jer. x. 10.) "The LORD is GOD, Who keepeth truth for ever," says David. (Ps. cxlvi. 6.)

He is *eternal.* As there never was a time when He was not, so will there never be a time when He will not be. He is the "Everlasting FATHER;" "of His kingdom there will be no end."

III.

THE HOLY TRINITY.

" There are three that bear record in heaven, the Father, the Word, and the Holy Ghost : and these three are one."—1 S. John v. 7.

THE doctrine of which I have to speak to you to-day is one hard to understand, but not hard to believe. I mean the doctrine of the Holy TRINITY.

We are called on to believe that in the one Godhead there are Three Persons,—the FATHER, the SON, and the HOLY GHOST. That the FATHER is GOD, the SON is GOD, and the HOLY GHOST is GOD ; and yet there are not three GODS, but one GOD.

Three in One, yet One in Three, dimly here we worship GOD. We acknowledge GOD the FATHER to be Almighty, GOD the SON to be Almighty, and GOD the HOLY GHOST to be Almighty ; and there are not three Almighties, but one Almighty.

There never was a time when GOD the FATHER was not. There never was a time when GOD the SON was not. There never was a time when GOD the HOLY GHOST was not. And yet there are not three Eternals, but one Eternal.

This is called the doctrine of the TRINITY.

As you see, this is hard to explain and to understand, but it is not hard to believe. A child can believe it, a philosopher cannot explain it.

But if I cannot explain this mystery to you, I think I can show you in nature certain figures whereby we may get some idea of how true the mystery is, though it is difficult for us to understand.

If I were to shut the window of a room, and cut a slit in the shutter, and insert a piece of glass called a prism, you would see on the wall on the other side of the room a streak of red, yellow, and blue light. If I take the piece of glass away, there is only a streak of white light. Now scientific men have found out that all pure white light is made up of red, yellow, and blue light; and by that piece of glass a ray of light can always be separated into the parts which make it up.

Now the red ray is light, the yellow ray is light, the blue ray is light. But the three together make up only one ray of light.

Then again. In your own self you have an image of the TRINITY. You are made up of mind, and body, and spirit or soul. The mind that thinks, the mind that is following what I am telling you, is *you*. You say, "I think, or, I don't think." You speak of your mind as your very self. Well, so is your body *you*. If any one runs a needle into your flesh, you start and say, "You are hurting me." You speak of your body as if it were yourself. Then your soul, or spirit, is *you*. When you have received some good impression from a sermon, you say, "It did me good." It did not affect your mind or your body. It only touched your soul. And you speak of your soul as if it were you yourself.

Well,—here there is the mind *you*, the body is *you*, and the soul is *you*. And yet you do not make up three individuals, but you make only one man.

Sometimes your mind urges one way, and your body another way. Sometimes your soul and your body are in opposition. S. Paul speaks of this which he felt. He says, "I delight in the law of GOD after the inward man,"—that is, in his mind,—"but I see another law in my members," —that is, in the passions of the body,—"warring against the law of my mind, and bringing me into captivity to the law of sin which is in my members." (Rom. vii. 22, 23.)

Now there is no such disagreement and discord between the Persons of the Godhead, but all three are perfectly one in will, and one in purpose. And when we enter into eternal life that disagreement and discord in our natures will have ceased, and the mind, and the soul, and the body will be united in purpose, as are the FATHER, and the SON, and the HOLY GHOST.

Perhaps I may make it a little more easy for you to understand this mystery if I show you another resemblance. Look at that window. In most ancient churches the east window, or one of the other windows, is so constructed as to teach the doctrine of the TRINITY.

Now observe that window well. It is made up of three parts, by two stone mullions which separate it into what are called three lights.

I send for a bricklayer and tell him to brick up the two outer lights. Then when he has plastered his brickwork over, and smoothed it like the rest of the wall, what will you call that which remains? You will call it a window, of course.

Now suppose I tell the bricklayer that he has made a mistake. I wish the right hand and the middle compartments of the window to be blocked up. He does so, and then what is that which remains, and through which the morning sun shines into the chancel? A window, of course.

But I change my mind, and tell the bricklayer to throw open the right hand compartment, and block up the left hand one as well as the middle one. He does so, and then what is that which remains? A window, of course.

So each portion of that window is in itself a window. That right hand compartment is a window. That middle compartment is a window. That left hand compartment is a window. And yet you would not say that there were three windows in the east wall of the church over the altar, but one window.

Now you can get some sort of idea how the FATHER can be GOD, the SON GOD, and the HOLY GHOST GOD, and yet that there should not be three GODS, but One GOD.

You know the florin, or two-shilling piece, that it has a cross of shields on one side. In the corners of that cross are flowers or plants. In the first and fourth are roses. The rose is the badge of England. In the second is the thistle; that is the badge of Scotland. In the third is a little cluster of clover leaves. The clover leaf, called in Irish the shamrock, is the badge of Ireland. I will tell you how the Irish obtained the clover leaf as their badge. Long ago, when the Irish were heathens, there came to their shores S. Patrick, to teach them the true Catholic faith. He was brought to the king, and he spoke before him of the religion of CHRIST. The king listened attentively.

But when S. Patrick began to tell him that there was but one God, and yet in that Godhead there were three Persons, the king stopped him, and said, " I do not understand you. You say the FATHER is GOD."

" Yes."

" And you say that the SON is GOD."

" Yes."

" And you say, that the HOLY GHOST is GOD."

" Yes."

" Then," said the king, " there must be three GODS."

S. Patrick stooped down, instead of answering, and picked a clover leaf which grew at his feet. The clover leaf is made up of three little leaves joined by a slim stalk together, so that the three leaves make only one leaf. As you go out of church pick a leaf in the churchyard and look at it. You will see what I mean.

S. Patrick held up only one of the lobes and said, " This is a leaf."

" Yes," said the king.

He showed the second lobe, and said, " This is a leaf."

" Yes," said the king.

He showed the third lobe, and said, " This is a leaf."

" Yes," said the king.

Then S. Patrick held the entire leaf up by its long stalk before the king, and said, " What is this ?"

" It is a leaf," answered the king.

"So learn from a humble plant the mystery of the TRINITY," said the saint.

I will give you one other illustration, and that is the sun. What is there in the sun that makes it up ? Light, heat, and body. The disk you see, and round which the world rolls, the light that makes our day, and which pours from it, and the heat which produces our summer, makes the plants spring, and which ripens the grain.

Now the sun pours forth light and heat. It produces the light and the heat, and there never was a time when the sun was without light and heat, as far as we know. The sun begets the ray of light, but the sun was not before the ray, nor are sun and ray before the heat. Thus there never was a time when the FATHER was without the SON, and the FATHER and SON without the HOLY GHOST.

This is not perhaps such a simple illustration as the others, and so I will not dwell on it any longer.

Now each Person of the TRINITY has a special function as regards man. GOD the FATHER we look upon as our Creator; GOD the SON as our Redeemer; GOD the HOLY GHOST as our Sanctifier.

The Creed is grouped into three parts, the part relating to GOD the FATHER, that relating to GOD the SON, and that relating to GOD the HOLY GHOST.

I shall speak to you of each of these in its turn, and explain to you, in order, how GOD the FATHER made us, how GOD the SON redeemed us, and how GOD the HOLY GHOST sanctifies us.

The truths I shall have to explain to you will be more easily understood by you than this of the TRINITY. But if more easily understood they are not to be regarded as more important. It is our ignorance and weakness of comprehension which makes us unable to understand fully the mystery of the TRINITY. A little bird, a fly, a worm cannot understand the nature of a man, our nature is so far above it. So the vastness of the distance between GOD's nature and our nature makes it impossible for us to fully comprehend GOD.

IV.

THE FATHER ALMIGHTY.

" Our Father, which art in heaven."—S. Matth. vi. 9.

GOD the FATHER is so called because He is the FATHER
of our LORD JESUS CHRIST the Second Person of the
TRINITY.

We do not mean that He is Father in the same way in
which a human father is parent of his child. We do not
mean that there ever was a time when the FATHER was
alone in heaven without the SON ; and that there ever was a
time when the SON came into existence. No. We speak
in these terms because we are obliged to apply words having
only a human signification to GOD, who is spiritual, and because we have no better words to use. We use the words
FATHER and SON, not to express that one is the author of
the being of the other, but to signify the relations of love
in which one stands to the other. Let me give you an illustration. All such illustrations must be imperfect, but still,
making allowance for this imperfection, they help us to realize
in some sort, the mysteries of our religion. You stand before
a looking-glass. Instantly you produce the exact image of
your person in the glass. You are the cause, the generator,
the father of that likeness. The likeness does not produce you, but you produce the likeness. The FATHER in
heaven through all eternity contemplating His perfections
begets eternally the SON, who is the express image of His
Person.

I will give you another illustration. The thought in your

mind begets the word, and what you say exactly represents
your thought : it is the express image of your thought.　So
JESUS CHRIST is in Scripture called the Word of GOD, as
standing to the FATHER in the same relation as the word
we speak does to the thought we frame.

Well, then, we call GOD the FATHER because He is the
FATHER of our LORD JESUS CHRIST.

But He is also the FATHER of all Christians, by adoption.
I mean this : all such people as become members of
JESUS CHRIST, through their union with JESUS CHRIST partake in His Sonship, and are therefore adopted into His
family.　If you have a son, and the son marries, his wife
becomes your daughter.　She is adopted into your family
by her union with your son.

There is a form by which this adoption into the family of
GOD is made, just as there is a form by which your son
makes a woman his wife, and that makes her to become
your daughter.　If your son was not married to the woman,
she could not claim you as her father; so unless we go
through the form which unites us to CHRIST, we are not
adopted into the family of GOD.　It would not be any good
for a woman to say, " I love your son very much, I believe
in him thoroughly.　I am sure I like him as much as if he
were my husband."　The mere fact of her liking and believing in him, and trusting him would not make her your
daughter.　It is the form of marriage which constitutes the
relationship, not the sentiment of the heart.

So is it with the relationship with GOD of which I am
speaking.　The form by which we are united to CHRIST,
so as to become members of Him, is Baptism.　If we are
baptized, we are at once children of GOD.　It is not believing in CHRIST, loving Him, trusting Him, which makes

us children of GOD, it is the having been baptized. That is the form which brings us at once into relationship to GOD as children to a father.

But again. Your son's wife may behave very badly, may cease to love him, and disobey him, and even desert him. But however badly she may behave, she is still your daughter. The relationship remains.

So, however badly baptized Christians may behave, however little they may love and obey CHRIST, even though they may desert Him, yet are they still children of GOD, though rebellious children.

The relationship still remains unaffected by the conduct of the children.

Of course I do not mean to say that baptized people will all inherit the privileges and glory promised to them, if they misconduct themselves. The promises of GOD are conditional; but the relationship is perpetual. Your own children may forfeit every right to the money you may have saved up, and which you intended to give them, so that instead of leaving it to them, you will leave it to their cousins, but you cannot alter their relationship to you. You cannot make your son not to be your son but your nephew, you cannot make your daughter not to be your daughter, but the child of other parents.

This then is the relation in which we stand to GOD, and now I will speak of the benefits attaching to that relation, and the conditions on which those benefits repose.

When we were adopted to be the children of GOD, we undertook certain things :—to believe revealed truth, and to do GOD's will. In order that we might be able to believe the truth, and do GOD's will, GOD then promised to give us His help, that is Grace ; and He also promised, if with the help of

Grace we kept our promise, that He would reward us with Eternal Life.

Mind. The benefits are conditional. The relationship is certain. We cannot alter our relationship, we can neglect our privileges and lose the benefits.

Suppose the squire were to adopt one of your children, and were to promise if the child behaved well, was loving and obedient, to leave it his fortune after he died. Suppose the child proved unruly, did all it could to vex and distress him, would it have any claim on his inheritance? No: it would have forfeited its inheritance.

In like manner we may lose that which we are promised at our baptism,—Eternal Life, if we do not keep our part of the covenant, fulfil our engagement, by believing the Catholic Faith, and keeping the Commandments of GOD.

GOD is also the FATHER of all things that He has made. He is their FATHER by creation. He called all things into being out of nothing. Therefore all look to Him as the Author of their being. Consequently He is the FATHER of every beast and bird and fish and flower. They all derive their life, their substance, and their powers from Him as from their FATHER.

He is also their FATHER as being their preserver. Just as a father looks after his children, and provides shelter and food and clothing for them, so does GOD look after the creatures He has made, and provides for their welfare. He gives the shelter of the tree to the bird for its nest, the burrow to the rabbit, the den to the lion. He provides for all their meat in due season, and gives each of His creatures the instinct or sagacity necessary to enable it to get its living. And He clothes all against the cold, He gives feather to the bird, hair to the dog, wool to the sheep, and to man, the most perfect of His creatures, He has given understanding which will serve him to find or construct a habitation, to procure his food, and fashion his clothing.

" The eyes of all wait upon Thee, O LORD! Thou openest Thy hand, and fillest all things living with plenteousness."

Thus, then, my brethren, we are GOD'S children by the fact of His having made us, having called us into being.

But this title to sonship is very inferior to that we derive from our being united to His dear SON. The highest sonship is a heavenly, divine relationship. It places us in a very special relationship to Him. It exalts the baptized into a position of favour with Him as high above the rest of men, as the rest of men are exalted above the brutes. It transfers us to a new realm, the kingdom of Grace. It puts us into an entirely new connection with Him, so that through His SON, we are made partakers of the Divine nature. When we are in the world, as merely His children by His creation and preservation of us, we are governed only by the laws of His temporal administration, that is the laws by which He governs the visible things of creation. But when we are made His children by adoption, we are translated into His spiritual kingdom, and are at once under new and heavenly influences, subject to new laws, with new powers and new privileges.

Suppose a negro slave in America were to escape in a ship to England. You know the saying that, when a slave touches English soil he is a free man. It is quite true. The moment he has set foot in England, he is free. In England the poor slave finds that he has acquired new rights, new privileges, new powers. When a slave, he had no right to his time, to his labour, even to his wife and children.

Here in England all are absolutely his own. As a slave he could not enter into any profession or trade, he could not invest his money, he could not distribute his money as pleased him, for he could not earn any money. Here in England he may earn money, perhaps make a fortune. It is his own, he may invest his money as he likes, he may leave it to whom he likes. As a slave he was beyond the pale of the law, here the law takes care of him, will not suffer any man to rob him or to wound him or to kill him. He has passed from one realm to another realm, and in so passing has entered into an entirely new condition of existence.

So it is with us. The moment we have passed the waters of baptism, and set our foot on the soil of the Catholic Church, we are free. We are in a new realm; we have passed into a spiritual kingdom, governed by spiritual laws, and given spiritual privileges.

In our former condition we might labour to do what was right, but we could not look for reward. In the kingdom of CHRIST all we do that is good is like so much treasure laid up. It makes a store of merit. It is rewarded, or paid for by GOD. In our former condition all our efforts were by our own strength. We had only our own desires after something better to fall back upon as a last resource. In the kingdom of CHRIST we have abundant spiritual assistance. GOD Himself helps our infirmities.

In our former condition we were isolate, that is, all by ourselves, each man shifting for himself, none could help another. "No man can deliver his brother, nor make agreement unto GOD for him;" says David. But in the kingdom of CHRIST all are bound together by spiritual brotherhood, and the ministry of one man is for the benefit of his brother, and the prayers of all are for the advantage of each.

"If one member suffer, all the members suffer with it ; or if one member be honoured, all the members rejoice with it. Now ye are the body of CHRIST, and members in particular." (1 Cor. xii. 26, 27.)

In our former condition if at the last Judgment we were proved to have been deficient, we should be cast out into eternal death. But in the kingdom of CHRIST the great treasury of the merits of CHRIST and His Saints is open to all, so that the abundant merits there can be made over to supply the deficiency of those that lack, and that earnestly desire salvation, though from ignorance, or error, they have gone astray from the right path, yet sincerely seek amendment ere it be too late : "That now at this time your abundance may be a supply for their want, that their abundance also may be a supply for your want." (2 Cor. viii. 14.)

If then GOD be our FATHER, what are the duties that we owe to Him as a FATHER?—Love and Obedience. Love, for that He has created us, and preserves us daily, that He has translated us out of darkness into the kingdom of His dear SON. Love to Him because we are His children by adoption and Grace. Love because of the exceeding precious promises He has made us, but, Oh ! surely for a higher motive still. "We love GOD, because He first loved us."

And I think, my brethren, if we can only have this love in us, there is no need of speaking at length on the subject of obedience, for He who loveth GOD keeps His Commandments. "This is the love of GOD, that we keep His Commandments." "This is love, that we walk after His Commandments."

V.

THE CREATION OF ANGELS.

"And there was war in heaven: Michael and his angels fought against the dragon; and the dragon fought and his angels, and prevailed not; neither was their place found any more in heaven. And the great dragon was cast out, that old serpent, called the Devil, and Satan, which deceiveth the whole world: he was cast out into the earth, and his angels were cast out with him."—Rev. xii. 7—9.

BEFORE GOD called into existence the world as we now see it, He had created angels.

Angels are pure spirits, with spiritual bodies. That is, they have not gross bodies which need food to keep them alive, which grow older, which are necessary for their moving from place to place. But their bodies are spiritual, they have all the faculties, such as sight, hearing, smelling, feeling, tasting, and also reason, memory, intelligence, which are not dependent on the supply of food and drink and exercise and wholesome air, as are those of our bodies. Our bodies are liable to be hurt, a knife will cut the flesh, a nail scratch the skin, fire will burn them. If we fell into the sea we should be drowned. But spiritual bodies are not liable to be hurt, no knife could hurt an angel's body, no nail would scratch it. An angel would be unhurt in the midst of a flame, and could dive to the bottom of the sea; water would not drown it.

A spiritual body, again, can travel as fast as thought. If you want to go to Colchester you have to walk ten miles, it takes you a long time, two hours and a half, or three hours. Why? Because you have only a natural body, and to get the natural body along, it must move its legs, and the legs will not travel except slowly. But a spiritual body is not thus inconvenienced. It thinks, and is there. If you had a spiritual body, you would think of Colchester, and the same instant you would be in Colchester. The act of thought would be the act of transport. So, in heaven, an angel has only to think of some place whither he is sent, and he is instantly there.

Now when GOD made the angels, He also gave them free wills. A Free Will means a will to obey GOD, or to disobey Him. Now stocks and stones, water, plants, fishes, birds, animals, have no free wills, they cannot disobey GOD, because they have no ideas other than just to do what they are created to do. A dog could never wish to act and live differently from what it is by nature, because it has no free will.

Now free will is a great privilege, and like all great privileges it entails a heavy responsibility. To have a free will is to partake of the Divine nature. The existence of imagination is to us a proof of the possession of free wills. We can imagine something different from what it is; and so we wish to be what we imagine so much better. For the thousands of years that the world has lasted, the idea of a kennel never entered a dog's head, and so dogs never set to work and made kennels. Men imagined that huts would be warm things to live in, so they built huts, then they imagined that they could improve their huts, so they built houses, and then went on furnishing and improving their houses till they became palaces.

It is the existence of this imagination and free will together which makes man such an active, progressive being.

If we had been without free wills we should have stuck at the same point where we had been created. We should never have imagined anything better, we should never have wished for anything better, and so have lived on like cabbages, or horses, or dogs, one generation after another, in one dead monotony of common uniformity.

But if there is an imagination to picture to us something good, and a will to wish for something better, the imagination may also picture something bad, and the will may wish for what is evil. That is to say, the free will may desire to fulfil GOD's will, or it may desire to oppose GOD's will. GOD's will is that His creatures should always do that which they were designed by Him to do. And He designed them that they might find perfect happiness. If one of His creatures wishes to do that which he was not designed for, then he meets with unhappiness. So keeping GOD's will means seeking perfect happiness, disobedience to GOD's will means finding misery. And having free wills, angels and men can do either.

GOD made your fingers tender, clothed in a very delicate skin. If you put them between the bars of the grate into the fire, you burn them, and are filled with pain. That is because you are doing with your fingers what GOD had not designed your fingers for. He did not make them fireproof, and if you will expose them to fire, you are going against what GOD willed for your fingers, and consequently suffer pain.

It is so with everything else. Sin is our going against GOD's will, wishing to be and do that which GOD did not make us to be or to do; and then doing those things for which we were not designed by GOD. GOD did not design and fashion you to cut somebody else's throat. He designed you, and sent you into the world to live in peace and do honest work. If you cut a man's throat you are doing that which you were not made for, going against GOD's will, and so bring suffering down upon your head.

Now to return to the Angels. GOD gave them free wills. That is to say, in one word, He made them perfect beings. At last, some of the angels, led by one of the archangels then named Lucifer, but now called Satan, set their wills against the will of GOD. They wished to be almighty. They wished to be and to do those things for which they were not created. Instantly the pangs of hell took hold of them. They had gone against their nature, and so necessarily suffered. They were cast out of heaven. But instead of repenting, that is, turning round and bending back their wills to agree with the will of GOD, and determining once more to occupy that place for which GOD had created them, they became more bitter in their opposition to GOD, they kept growing more at war in their wishes with what GOD had willed them to be. And because they could only be happy in that condition in which GOD had placed them, they daily suffered more anguish, the more they separated themselves from their predestined condition and true vocation.

Let me give you a very rough and homely illustration. You have a son whom you destine for the land like yourself, as a farm labourer; you have brought him up to mind horses, and to know all that is necessary for farm service. He runs away to sea. You know what that means here. It happens often enough. And sometimes the boys find that they cannot get on at sea at all, they are always unwell with the least motion of the vessel. Some get over it very soon, but some never do; and the captain finding them to be useless as sailors sends them back to be landsmen. Now, what if one of these lads, the one I am speaking of, was miserable at sea; never could get accustomed to it; found it daily more detestable, and yet to vex and disappoint his father would not return. He would be following a manner of life he was not destined to, and which he was not suited for, and so was miserable; but still his pride and bad passion prevent him from returning to his obedience, and to a life for which he is suited, and so recovering his happiness and health.

This will give you some notion of what the devils did. They were once obedient children of GOD in heaven. But they would be something other than what GOD purposed, and so they became miserable, and they are now more set against GOD and that which they were destined for than ever before, and so they continue miserable.

It is the same with us. If we will do that which GOD does not intend us to do, we go to destruction and misery. We are like a train that gets off its line of rails, and you know what becomes of it. Whenever you commit sin you get off the rails, and if you do not get on again pretty sharp it will be all up with you.

GOD, then, had created the angels, and some of them rebelled against Him, and were cast into endless misery. But the rest of the angels remained faithful, they wished for nothing that was not in agreement with GOD's will, and so found happiness.

Now when Satan and his host of rebels were cast out of heaven, there was left a great gap in the ranks of the blessed creatures of GOD.

To fill this gap GOD created man. He created them perfect, that is, with free wills to serve Him and find happiness if they liked, to disobey Him and find woe if they liked. Mankind fell in its first parents, and CHRIST came on earth to restore mankind. Of that I shall speak hereafter.

Suffice it now to say that our happiness depends on our exercising our free wills in the direction of that which is right, just as our misery depends on our exercising our free wills in the direction of that which is wrong. Your son, who is at sea, and is always ill there, remains away from you and happiness by an exercise of his will. He won't return to the path of duty. The devils remain in hell because they won't return to obedience to GOD. Hell will receive you at the last if you remain obstinately opposed to the service of GOD. You know how bad people after having gone on sinning hate what is good. Idle good-for-nothing fellows, who go loafing about our country parishes, frequenting the pot-house, and never working steadily anywhere, hate the decent orderly workman who is regular in all he does, and lives in sobriety. This fellow is miserable himself, his bed is without a blanket, his children without boots, his cupboard without a loaf. And he would like to see all you decent steady men as wretched and discontented as himself. He hates regular work. He hates steadiness. He hates temperance.

I have seen wicked old gentlemen who have lived lives of debauchery, delight in demoralizing young men out of downright hatred of innocence. You may know what a limb of Satan a wicked old woman is who has led a disorderly life, and how dangerous her tongue and advice are to young girls. That is because these aged sinners hate virtue, simplicity, and purity. A drowning man tries to drag under water the man who is swimming; so a sinking sinner tries to pull others down to hell with him.

The devils have also a spite against us men and women, because they know that we were created to fill up their places in heaven. They know that the happiness which was theirs is offered to us. Therefore they are jealous of us, and they do all in their power to spoil our happiness, to prevent us from getting to heaven.

If, when your son went to sea, so disobediently, you adopted another boy in his place, and then having made a large fortune were to promise it all to the adopted son, what would the seaman think of the lad who was chosen in his place? Would he not hate him? I think if he came ashore he would do all in his power to injure him, and if he were not afraid of the laws would kill him.

Well, so the devils hate us. To each one of you is offered a mansion in heaven which belonged once to a devil; imagine the spite that devil bears you! No wonder he tries to destroy you.

So now you see why there are evil spirits, and why these evil spirits are in league against you. Take care that you do not let them rob you of your prize! Take care that you do not let them blind you to your true happiness, and, by drawing you away from the service of GOD, rob you of your inheritance, and bring down on you an eternity of woe!

VI.

ON GUARDIAN ANGELS.

"*Are they not all ministering spirits, sent forth to minister for them who shall be heirs of salvation ?*"—Hebrews i. 14.

IN my last Sermon I spoke to you so fully of the devils that I had not much space for speaking to you about the Angels. I told you that heaven had been full of angels, but that some were disobedient, and these had been cast out of heaven, and that the disobedient angels are called devils. I told you also why men were created, to fill the void caused by the fall of the angels. I told you also how that the fact of man's creation to fill this void leagued all the devils against us. Not only do they hate us for our goodness, when there is goodness in us, but also they hate us, as Esau hated Jacob, because we supplant them.

Now to-day, I am going to speak to you about the good angels, and their mission.

GOD, seeing us led away by our fallen nature and passions, and drawn on to evil by the devils, has commissioned His good angels to minister to us for good, that we may not be left at the mercy of the devils. GOD wills our salvation, that is, our happiness ; it was for *that* that He created us, but Adam, by willing something contrary to the will of GOD, fell, and all his race fell with him. As GOD wills our happiness, the holy angels, who will only what GOD wills, desire our happiness also, and therefore labour to draw us to that which is good, just as the devils labour to draw us to that which is evil.

D

S. Paul says that they are ministering spirits sent forth to minister for all them who shall be heirs of salvation. Here we learn something which is very important, viz., whom the angels are commissioned to serve, and when they are sent to serve.

We are made heirs of salvation at our baptism. Heirs of salvation means inheritors of the kingdom of heaven, as it is called in the catechism. At our baptism GOD promises to us, conditionally, that happiness which we lost by the fall of Adam. As soon as we are made heirs, at once angels are sent to minister to us. They alone who are heirs, they, that is, alone, who have been made heirs by baptism, are sure of having angels to minister to them.

If we had spiritual sight to see spiritual things, at every baptism we should see an angel sail down out of heaven, and take its stand by the baptized. There is a little baby yonder in its mother's arms whom I baptized not so very long ago. As we were standing at the font we were four at the beginning of the baptism, four with the child, three godparents and myself. As soon as the drops of water rested on the child's brow we were five. An angel had taken his place at the font, sent from GOD out of heaven to be the guardian of that child through life, and to bear its soul away at death.

O, my brethren! if we could only see with spiritual sight, we should behold a number of angels here, one standing by each of us, my angel is here with his wings above me in the pulpit, an angel watches each of you in your seats.

Do you think it impossible that your eyes should see such things? There are a good number of men in this world who cannot see colours. A friend was staying with me last week: as we were walking in the garden he pointed to a peony, and said, "Is there any difference between the colour of the flower and that of the leaves? I can see none." To me it seems perfectly impossible to confuse the blood crimson flower with the dark green leaves. I cannot understand it. Look at the altar cloth, that man would not be able to tell you whether it were red or green.

I dare say an angel is just as much puzzled how it is that you cannot see him. It seems to him quite inexplicable.

Now GOD might at any time make the little difference in the eye which would enable it to distinguish colours, so that the colour-blind man might for a minute see the blueness of the sky, and the green of the grass, and the yellow of the dandelion, and the pink of the red-robin in the hedges. So GOD may, and I feel sure does, at times enable the eye to see spiritual beings, to get a glimpse of angels. We read of several instances of the kind in the Bible, and we are often hearing of them occurring now-a-days. I have read a story of a very holy woman, named S. Frances of Rome, who was called on to suffer most grievous afflictions. She lost a darling little boy. It was a bitter pang to her, added to very many others. But GOD gave her in exchange this very power of which I am speaking. From that moment she was allowed to see her guardian angel, and never after, till the day of her death, was she deprived of the sight of him. She thus described the angel: "His stature is that of a child of about nine years; his countenance full of sweetness and majesty; his eyes generally turned towards heaven. Words cannot describe the divine purity of that gaze. His brow is always serene; his glances kindle in the soul the flame of burning devotion. When I look upon him, I understand the glory of the angel's nature, and the degraded condition of our own. He wears a long shining robe, and over it a tunic, either as white as the lilies of the field, or of the colour of the red rose, or of the hue of the sky when it is most deeply blue. When he walks at my side his feet are never soiled by the mud of the streets, or the dust of the roads." The presence of her heavenly guide was to her as a mirror, in which she saw reflected every imperfection of her character. When she committed any fault the angel faded away; and it was only when she had felt very sorry and had confessed her fault, that he shone out upon her once more in all his brilliancy.

Now I do not for one moment believe that this holy woman told a lie about all this. I know that such guardians are sent to minister to those who are heirs of salvation, and I know so many cases of persons whom I can trust who say they have seen them, that I should be very wrong in doubting it. When my mother was very ill, before her death, she often told me she could see her angel beside her bed, and when she could not speak much, if I went on one side of the bed, she used to beckon me to the other side, saying, " Not on that side, the angel is there."

I have read a story of a very good ploughman. He used to go to church to pray every day at day-break, and then hurry to his work. His master was told that the man did not come in time, so he went one morning early to see if the man was ploughing. And there in the dawning light the farmer saw his labourer at the plough running it up and down the field, and a white angel gliding beside him. I do not disbelieve the story. If GOD opened the eyes of Elisha's servant, He might have opened those of this farmer.

The guardian angel, sent by GOD to minister to us heirs of salvation, is with us all our lives. Think of this, my dear friends! when you are in the field ploughing, the angel is by your side. When you come home in the evening, the angel glides along behind you. When you sit down to your meals, the angel is behind your chair. When you lie down to sleep, the angel spreads his wings over your bed. When you pray, the angel bears your supplications up to GOD. When you die, the angel takes your soul to paradise.

How then should you behave in the presence of this blessed companion? How think you he likes to hear evil words proceed out of your mouth? or to see you do that which is wrong? Do you not think a bright and beautiful smile breaks out on his face when you do that which is good, that a glad beam kindles his eye when you kneel to pray?

There is this thought to bear in mind. It is quite possible for us to drive the angel away. If we continue in sin till all power of wishing for a better life, all desire of good, is dead in us, till we are wholly given over to a reprobate mind, then the angel sadly spreads his wings and leaves the guilty soul, recalled from such an unprofitable work by GOD.

There is a passage in our LORD's teaching which bears on the doctrine of the holy angels, which I did not always understand, till it was explained to me by a poor uneducated man. After our LORD had said how terrible will be the punishment of those who injure the souls of little children, He adds, "In heaven their angels do always behold the face of My FATHER which is in heaven."

One night, when I was a young man, before I was in holy orders, I was walking in Devonshire, along a lane, and I caught up a walking postman ; and as we were both going along in the same direction we walked together and fell into conversation. Presently the road came out on a wild moor covered with rocks, and far from any habitation. I said to

the man, "Are you never alarmed, travelling along such a
desolate road, and in such a wild country, and almost always
alone?" "No," he answered; "not now."

I pressed him for his reason, and then he said, "I used
to be frightened at times, of a night, for there are strange
tales of these moors; but one Sunday, our parson preached
at church on the ministry of the holy angels. He told us
how an angel was sent by GOD to minister to each one of the
baptized, and to be with him to the end of life. I have often
thought of that, and it struck me much. So when I have
been alone of a dark night I think that my angel is beside
me, and sometimes I pray, and sometimes I sing a hymn,
and I like to think that the angel joins with me. I don't
know that I hear his voice, but it seems to me sometimes
as if I did. And then I speak to him, and I feel that I
have a companion, and it takes all loneliness away."

After some talk, we came to speak of the text, "In
heaven their angels do always behold the face of My FA-
THER which is in heaven," and I told him that it was not
intelligible to me; for that angels did not mean the souls of
the children.

"No," said he; "I've thought of that text, and this is
what I fancy it means. The angels of little children always
see the face of GOD, they are always looking up to GOD,
like this." The man's face was raised, and the full moon
shone on it, lighting it up brightly. "But it is not so
always; presently sin comes, bad example from parents or
companions produces an evil act, and then a cloud comes
between the face of GOD and the angel." As the man was
speaking, with his eyes raised, an arm of black cloud stole
across the moon, and a shadow fell on his face, and it was
only dimly visible. "Like this," continued the postman;

"and if sin continues growing more and more, it is like a bank of black cloud coming up and obscuring entirely the face of GOD, so that all is dark below. That is why woe is pronounced against him that leads a little one into sin, he darkens the angel's face, and then the guardian angel of the child arms himself to be an avenging angel against the man that has done evil."

Now remember what I told you about S. Frances of Rome. Her angel seemed to fade away when she sinned, and brighten again when she repented. Is not that like what the postman thought? When the face of GOD shone on the angel, S. Frances saw him, when the face of GOD was obscured by her sin, he faded from sight. You must have noticed sometimes in a wood how a beam of sun striking in among the trees touches a spray of leaves, or perhaps a tuft of flowers, and they are bright and distinct. The sun sets, and you cannot distinguish the spray and the flowers from other sprays and flowers, and all their beauty seems gone. So was it with the angel, the favour of GOD was light, and joy, and beauty. When that was obscured all faded from sight.

And now I will say no more, except to urge you not to forget the presence of your angel, so as never to offend him voluntarily, and darken him through your sins.

VII.

THE CREATION AND FALL OF MAN.

" As by one man sin entered into the world, and death by sin ; so death passed upon all men, for that all have sinned."—Rom. v. 12.

I HAVE already told you for what purpose GOD made man. He made man to take the place of the fallen angels.

He made man to be perfectly happy. Happiness was what GOD had predestined to every man. That he might enjoy beautiful sights, GOD gave him eyes to see, and created lovely flowers, beauteous forms, colours, landscapes, and, in a word, all that can delight the eye. That he might enjoy sweet sounds, GOD gave man ears to hear, and arranged that certain vibrations of the air should produce a charming effect on his ears ; He gave song to the birds, and adapted the voice of men to sing, and ordained certain things as serviceable for making into musical instruments. That man might receive pleasure from scent, GOD gave him a sense of smell, and created the jessamine, the rose, the mignionette, and the honeysuckle. That he might take pleasure in taste, GOD gave him a discerning palate, and created the grape, and the peach, the apple, and cherry, and all pleasantly tasted things for food. And so with touch also.

Then He gave to man intelligence, and a love of acquiring knowledge, and to delight that He made creation full of endless variety and interest, so that men are ever studying GOD's works and never coming to an end, "for His thoughts are very deep."

I do not mean that the world was made only for men. It was made for angels as well to be their delight; and I dare say that an angel is quite as full of pleasure at lighting on some new fair flower, as would be any man. But in an angel, as in a good man, the sight of some lovely thing would not merely gratify the sense, but would make the spirit swell and mount with thankfulness to GOD. I think that is the great thing which distinguishes the pleasure we obtain from lovely things that GOD has made from that which we derive from beautiful things man has made. The first is far the fullest happiness, because it is mixed with gratitude, the heart looks up, and that satisfies it, whereas in the other case it looks to man before it turns to GOD.

Understand then, that GOD made man to be happy. Loving man that He had made, He surrounded him with all that could delight him, and gave him faculties for enjoying everything.

But Adam and Eve, the first parents of our race, by an act of free will transgressed GOD's commandment. There was one thing He had forbidden, that one thing they did. They did not know evil before Satan tempted them to acquire a knowledge of it; and when once the knowledge of evil came into their minds, then the wish to do evil rose in them by a strange perversity. Directly they had gone against GOD's will, and acquired that knowledge which GOD had not designed them to acquire, then the shadow fell on their hitherto bright lives, and darkened all their future. Pain and death followed sin as its natural consequences, just as a smash is the consequence of a train leaping off the rails ; just as wreck is the result of a ship running on land. A train is made to run on rails, a ship is made to sail in water, man was made to live in innocence. In innocence was his

safety, in innocence his happiness. He left the condition
God had placed him in, and by leaving it lost his innocence
and wrecked his felicity.

You know how happy little children are. I think there
is no sweeter sight than children playing in a meadow in
spring, picking and twining the flowers. It is all sunlight
in those little hearts. As they grow older they learn to
know sin, and as the knowledge of sin enters, their lives
darken, the freshness of childhood languishes, the joyousness of youth dies away.

Often the knowledge of evil makes the wish to taste of
the evil grow in their hearts, and then the evil is done, and
so the darkness deepens on them, and lightheartedness dis-
appears. Parents I think of this, and keep your dear little
ones from the knowledge of evil,—so long they are in Paradise. Gradually Eden fades in the distance, as they advance
in life; then turn their eyes to it in the future, and convert
the regret into an aspiration.

The result of the fall of Adam and Eve was that the
original joyousness of man's heart was lost. It could only
go along with innocence.

Next it injured all his faculties, disordered and confused
them, so that the heart would wish this, whilst the mind
advised the contrary, and mind, soul and body would be at
discord.

Another effect of the Fall is that man is unable to educate
and perfect all his nature here. I mean that there is no
time for man to perfect more than one part of his nature in
this life. He has only time to attend to one thing, owing
to the struggle he has to maintain for his existence. For
instance, each one of you has all sorts of powers in you
which have never been brought out. Circumstances have

obliged you to devote all your attention to one sort of work,
the work of the farm.   There are plenty of other things
your minds might have been educated for, you might have
become skilful artists, your sense of the beautiful in nature
might have been brought out.   That would have required
you to turn all your attention to the shapes and colours of
things, and the play of light and shade.   But you have had
no time for that, your attention could not be fixed on two
things at once, and so it was turned to practical matters,
instead of to the beauty of creation.

The other day I was with a friend in the lane leading
down to the sea, the sun had set, and there was a most magnificent display of colour in the western sky.   It was one
of the most beautiful sunsets I have ever seen.   My friend
and I stood watching it, neither speaking, we were so full
of delight.   Close to us in the lane were three women with
a basket of clothes they had been washing.   They were
talking about the clothes, and the mending they would require.   I do not believe that they saw the sunset, or that,
if they had seen it, they would have found in it anything to
admire.   Here then were two finding a delight in the beauty
of creation, because from childhood up we had given our attention to it, and there were three who took a strong interest
in the washing and mending of the clothes, but none in the
sunset, because from childhood up they had given their
attention to washing and mending.

My friend and I knew nothing of what interested them,
and cared not for it.   Life is short, and it is impossible for
all to pay attention to everything.   Then among those who
love GOD's works, some are obliged to study only one
branch of creation, flowers, another insects, another birds,
and so on.   Life is too short for them to study all, dearly

as they would like. Then again, if my friend and I had been taken into a manufactory to see the various beautiful pieces of machinery, we should probably have felt no interest in it, because our attention has never been turned to machinery. I wish I did understand it, but alas! life is short, I have not time to study it.

So you see we go down to our graves only half, or quarter perfected beings, there are ever so many faculties in us which have become dormant, put away, as it were, on a shelf, because we have not time to use them. Not because we do not wish to use them, but we have no time, and the stress of circumstances prevents us from being able to employ them. Please GOD we may come to eternal life, and then we shall have plenty of time for making use of all our faculties, and growing, and growing, through endless time, wiser in every branch of knowledge, more delighting in every form of beauty.

I am not very sure that you can understand what I have been speaking about to-day, and follow what I have been trying to explain to you; and so I will put it in a shape that you cannot mistake.

GOD made man to be perfectly happy, and perfectly happy man could only be by obeying GOD. Adam and Eve disobeyed GOD, and so lost their original happiness. By their sin they brought in pain and death. All diseases are the result of sin having come into the world. The wages of sin is death.

Next, if we are to arrive at perfect happiness again, we must do the opposite to what Adam did, we must obey GOD. If we obey GOD's will, we are certain to find happiness, because then we are doing that we were made for. We must therefore make up our minds determinately to do GOD's

will. By an act of our will we must gain that which Adam lost by an act of his will. He chose to disobey GOD; we must choose to obey GOD.

But, unfortunately, this is not all. One of the results of the Fall is, that we are left so weak that we cannot of our own selves carry our resolution into effect. We are like men who have broken one of their legs, who struggle up and try to walk, but cannot get on unless a friend gives them an arm, or a stick, to help them on.

JESUS CHRIST gives us that which we want to assist us along. He gives us heavenly help, to enable us to do that which we have willed to do. His help is called Grace. I shall speak to you in another sermon about Grace, and how it helps us, and the relation in which it stands to our free wills.

But in conclusion, I ask you to bear away with you this lesson : your happiness here and hereafter depends on your bringing your wills into obedience to the Will of GOD. GOD's Will is enshrined in the Ten Commandments. "If thou wilt enter into life keep the Commandments."

VIII.

CHRIST THE TEACHER.

" The dayspring from on high hath visited us, to give light to them that sit in darkness and in the shadow of death, to guide our feet into the way of peace."—S. Luke i. 78, 79.

I HAVE told you that man who had been created perfectly good by GOD, and had been predestined,—that is, ordained and set apart for perfect happiness,—fell into sin and thereby lost his happiness.

I told you also that happiness can be recovered by man if he does that which GOD made him for, and willed him to do.

But in order that man may recover the happiness he had lost, he must know how to do so; he must be taught what is the will of GOD, the law of his nature.

Not only must men know what is the will of GOD, but they must also have help to observe it, for owing to the fall they are so weak, that however much they may wish to keep GOD's law, without help they cannot keep it.

Now perhaps you begin to see why CHRIST came into the world. He came to *teach* and to *help*. He came to teach men what GOD's law is, and to help them to observe it, when they have learnt what it is.

First He came to teach.

The descendants of Adam fell further and further from the knowledge and service of GOD, till at last, throughout the world, the greatest ignorance prevailed on three most important points which it behoved all men to know, the Nature of GOD, the Will of GOD, the Destiny of Man.

First then, as to the Nature of GOD.

We know that GOD is infinitely holy and just and good. But men in the olden times, before CHRIST came, did not know this. You read in your Old Testament of how parents passed their children through the fire to Moloch. That was the name of a god of the heathen, and the poor heathen thought him a cruel god, who revenged himself on men unless they gave him dreadful sacrifices. So they made great fires round the foot of the brazen statue of Moloch, and the brazen figure got hotter and hotter, as the flames licked it. The statue had its hands spread out over the flames. And when they were glowing, then the heathen priests took little babies and put them on the red-hot hands of the god, and they shrieked and rolled off into the flames beneath.

In our own land, before the Gospel was preached in it, the ancient Britons used to make great wicker-work figures, as tall as a house, to represent one of their gods, and then they took the prisoners they had captured in war, and put them inside the wicker-work figures, and burned them in it as a sacrifice to their god.

In Mexico, when the Spaniards discovered it, they found that human sacrifices were offered to the gods in the most horrible manner. The mode of sacrifice was the slicing open of the breast, and the tearing out of the still palpitating heart, which was then put to the lips of the god, after which the priests devoured the victim. At the dedication of a single Mexican temple 70,000 men were slaughtered. In Colchester there are 34,000 people. Imagine at the opening of one heathen place of worship more than twice as many people as there are in Colchester being butchered to please a false god. When the Spaniards entered the city of Mexico they found a pyramid of skulls, and they counted 136,000 heads. All these had been sacrificed to the god.

There are dreadful things going on in the world still, in honour and worship of false gods. But all these horrors sprang out of ignorance of the nature of GOD. The poor heathen people did not know what GOD's nature was; they thought, because some of their own kings were cruel, and GOD was greater than their kings, that therefore GOD was still more cruel.

We know that GOD is everywhere present.

The people in the olden time thought that He dwelt in an image, that is an idol, and so they worshipped the idol. Sometimes they thought He lived in the shape of a beast, and so they worshipped the beast.

I will read you what S. Clement, a great Christian bishop of Alexandria, says of the heathen temples in Egypt in his day : " The sanctuaries of the temples are covered with veils of gold tissue ; but if you advance towards the end of the temple, and look about for the statue, a minister of the temple advances with a grave air, chanting a hymn, and raises the veil a little, to show you the god. Then what do you see ? A cat, a crocodile, a serpent, or some other dangerous animal ! The god of the Egyptians appears ! it is a wild beast wallowing on a purple carpet."

So you see people did not in the least know what the nature of GOD was ; how then was it likely that they should know what His will is ?

You must bear in mind that unless men keep the will of GOD, happiness is not theirs. How then could they attain to happiness if they knew not the will of GOD ? They went on becoming wretched, seeking happiness in sins more and more horrible, with a fierce hunger in their souls for happiness, trying first this and then that to satisfy their longing for peace, and rest, and joy, and finding only misery and despair. Some thought that GOD's will was that they should commit the most atrocious crimes. There is at present a religious body of people in India, called Thugs, who believe that it is the will of GOD that they should strangle all men who do not think as they do ; and for many years the murders they committed to please their god were numerous. Now Government has put them down. In olden times, and even now, in India, worse things even, of unspeakable loathsomeness, have formed, and form still part of the religion of certain heathen bodies, thinking that by so doing they are fulfilling the will of GOD.

And as to their moral life, they do not know for certain that GOD wills them to be honest, chaste, truthful, temperate ; many of them think GOD wills them to be just the contrary.

Then again, as regards the destiny of man.

We know that GOD has made man to serve Him, and in serving Him to find eternal happiness. This is all news to the rest of the world. Before CHRIST came, men did not know for what they were sent into the world, and what would happen to them when they went out of the world. They thought that they had nothing set them to do here, that they might do right or wrong, it did not matter, that they might follow their pleasures, it did not matter, that whether they were honest, truthful, and pure, or thieves, liars, and adulterers, it did not matter, beyond the grave all was dark ; they had no certainty that they would live after death, no assurance that their future condition depended on their present life. They had no motive to make them try to be good, as far as their light went, and avoid doing wrong, as their passions led them.

As the world was in this dreadful condition of ignorance as to the Nature of GOD, the Will of GOD, and the Destiny of Man,—the three things man must know if he is to recover the happiness lost by the Fall, GOD the FATHER sent His only-begotten SON, JESUS CHRIST, very and Eternal GOD, into the world to teach the world,—to tell men what the Nature of GOD is, that He is holy, just, true, everywhere present, almighty, eternal.

E

To tell men what the Will of GOD is, that men should love GOD with all their hearts, with all their souls, and with all their might, and that they should love their neighbours as themselves.

To teach men what the Destiny of Man is. That GOD had created man for eternal happiness; and that eternal happiness was to be won by man bringing his will into agreement with the will of GOD. That GOD had appointed a certain day, in which He would judge all men by JESUS CHRIST, whom He had sent, for all that they had done in the body, that those who had done good should enter into heaven, and those who had done evil should be cast into hell.

Many hundreds of years ago, there came a Christian priest named Paulinus, to one of the kings of England. England was at that time broken up into several kingdoms, and was for the most part heathen. Paulinus asked the king to give him permission to preach the truth of CHRIST in his country. The king hesitated. Then a rough old nobleman said, " Oh, king! as we are sitting in this hall in winter, and it is night without, we have a blazing log-fire on the hearth in the middle, which lights up the hall. Then I have sometimes seen a little swallow come in at the door from the black night outside, and flutter and dart about in the light of the fire. Presently it skims out at one of the windows into the night and storm without. Whence that swallow came and whither it goes we know not. So it is with us. We are here in the light of life for a little while, born into the world, and dying out of it, but whence we came and whither we go we know not. If this stranger can tell us, by all means let us listen to him."

This then is what we have been taught by JESUS CHRIST,

the SON of GOD, and now there is no excuse for us remaining in ignorance as to the Nature of GOD, the Will of GOD, and the Destiny of Man.

This is what the world longed to know. It was not enough that prophets came and spake. The world would not listen to prophets, for how could mere men declare fully what was the nature of the invisible GOD? How could mere men teach authoritatively what was the will of an all holy GOD? How could mere men know certainly what GOD had made men for, and what He had prepared for them after death?

No, GOD Himself must teach men, for GOD alone could teach the whole truth. Therefore GOD sent forth His SON, born of a woman, into this dark and ignorant world, to enlighten its darkness, and to banish its ignorance.

"Glory to GOD in the highest, and on earth peace, good will towards men!" Well might the angels sing this glad strain, for GOD in His compassion had come down on earth to bring "light to them that sat in darkness and in the shadow of death, and to guide our feet into the way of peace."

IX.

CHRIST THE HELPER.

"Grace and Truth came by Jesus Christ."—S. John i. 17.

I HAVE already shown you how the Truth came by JESUS CHRIST. I must now explain to you how Grace comes by Him also.

But in order to do this properly, I must give you some instructions on the nature of our LORD JESUS CHRIST.

GOD the SON, equal in power and wisdom to the FATHER, came into the world to teach men the truth and to help men to believe and act upon the truth He taught. Now in order to teach and help, it was necessary He should be able to put the truth before men in such a way as they could understand it, and that He should be able to give help to them in such measure and manner as they would need it.

It was for this purpose that He took man's nature upon Him in the womb of the blessed Mary. He did not lay aside His Godhead that He might become man, but He joined the manhood to the Godhead. He did not give up the perfection of His nature as GOD when He took on Him the nature of man ; but He joined the perfection of the Godhead to the imperfection of the manhood. He did not give up His will as GOD when He took on Him the human will, but He united both in one. Nor did the Divine will overwhelm and destroy the human will, but subsisted beside it ; as the drooping flower is tied up to the stake to support and straighten it, so was the weak human will sustained and strengthened by the will of GOD.

When you want to explain something to a little child you put yourself into the place of the child as far as you can, and bring down your mind to its level, you try to understand what its difficulties are by an effort of surrender of your experiences. If you spoke to the little thing as you would to your wife, it would not understand you. So if I were to explain to you the mysteries of Christianity in the language of Theology, that is the science of religion, you would go away as wise as when you came here. I have to bring down these high thoughts to the level of your ideas.

Thus, when GOD the SON came to teach men, it would not do for Him to speak according to the ideas of GOD, and express the thoughts of GOD as they are in the mind of GOD. He became man, that He might translate the great thoughts of GOD into the narrow ideas of men. If you went to France, and spoke to the people in English, they would not understand you, you must turn your words into French, and then it is all plain to them. So CHRIST, by becoming man, turned the ideas of GOD into the ideas of men, so as to make these plain to men, and understandable by men.

Again :—Our LORD JESUS CHRIST took man's nature upon Him in order that He might be perfectly able to help us. By becoming man He was able to feel what our needs are, and show us that He has had experience of our necessities, so that we may with confidence look to Him as a helper. "Ye have not an high-priest which cannot be touched with the feeling of our infirmities ; but was in all points tempted like we are, yet without sin ; let us therefore come boldly unto the throne of grace, that we may obtain mercy, and find grace to help in time of need." (Heb. iv. 15, 16.)

This is an immense consolation to us. We know that CHRIST can feel for us, by the most certain proof; for we know that He suffered as we do. Are we sore pressed with spiritual or fleshly temptation ? So was He. Are we suffering weariness ? So did He. Are we in pain of body ? So was He. Are we in anguish of mind ? So was He. In every case He knows what pangs afflict us, He knows how far our feeble human natures can endure, and as our weakness is, so is His strength supplied. He gives grace to help in time of need.

Again :—in order that we may attain eternal happiness,

it is necessary, as I said before, and indeed have repeated over and over again, that we should obey GOD's will. But to obey GOD's will we must be induced by some motive. Now one motive, and that a very powerful one, is that we may attain happiness. But after all, this is a selfish motive. We do GOD's will for our own sake, that we may be better off in the end. We are not murderers, adulterers, thieves, because it will not pay in the long run. This is a motive, but it is not a very high one.

The highest, purest, and best motive for obeying GOD's will is love. If we love GOD we shall do His will. It will be pain and grief to us to be in disobedience, because it is estranging us from Him Who loveth us with an everlasting love, and Whom we love also because He loved us.

Now in order to give us every possible reason for loving Him, GOD has done all that He could possibly do to prove to us His love. If we do not love Him for the fair world He has made, we shall love Him for having redeemed us. CHRIST's coming on earth and taking man's nature upon Him, is an evidence to us that GOD loveth us. CHRIST, the only-begotten SON of GOD, Eternal and Almighty GOD Himself, consented to become man, to feel the pains of babyhood, the troubles of boyhood, the vexations of manhood, the pangs of death, to prove to us how dear we are to Him, how He withholds nothing from us, in His desire to exhibit His sympathy for us and with us.

A great historical writer who was describing the retreat of the French from Moscow, in order that he might be able vividly to present before his own mind and that of his readers the distress of the French army, spent one snowy night outside his house in his orchard. The Great Napoleon in that fatal retreat deserted his army, perishing with cold and hunger, and escaped to France where he could be snug, and warm. How indignant his soldiers must have felt. He had brought them into peril and misery, and then he ran away and left them in it, to secure his own comfort and safety. But suppose Napoleon had been in Paris, and his army was in sore distress in Russia, struggling through the deep snow, one soldier after another falling stark frozen on the ground. Suppose, hearing of this, he had rushed from the ease and comfort of his palace, into the wild snow waste of Russia, to be with his men in their peril and distress. What enthusiasm, what love he would have awakened in their hearts !

Now we are in great and sore distress, through our own fault, in going against the orders of our King. We have rebelled against Him, and in our rebellion have fallen into a piteous plight of misery. What is our King's course now? He rushes to the rescue—to the rescue of the rebels, with more than twelve legions of angels accompanying Him. He comes into the midst of us, and suffers with us, endures all the miseries we brought on ourselves by our rebellion, and all the while He is working our deliverance, bringing us up out of our difficulties, leading us into safety.

Well may we say with S. Francis Xavier, the Apostle of the Indies :—

> "My GOD, I love Thee ;—not because
> I hope for heaven thereby,
> Nor yet because who love Thee not
> Must burn eternally.
>
> "Not with the hope of gaining aught,
> Nor seeking a reward ;
> But as Thyself hast loved me
> O ever-living LORD.

"So would I love Thee, dearest LORD,
And in Thy praise will sing
Solely because Thou art my GOD
And my Eternal King."

CHRIST took human flesh also in order to be a Mediator between GOD and man. Partaking of both natures, being GOD and man, He unites both. Sin separated GOD and man. GOD and man are reunited in CHRIST. You may observe near the sea some stagnant pools of water, they are cut off from the sea by banks of mud. They are foul, swarming with hideous insects of all descriptions. Cut through the mud-bank, and the tide flows into them, gradually cleanses them, the black water grows pure and clear, the foul creatures disappear, and are replaced by forms of beauty, fair shells gleam out of the crystal depths, delicate crimson and green sea-weeds wave in the transparent water, and silvery fishes dart about therein. Mankind was that stagnant pool, CHRIST is the channel of communication between it and the pure deep ocean of the Godhead, and through Him the Divine nature ripples into human nature, cleansing it, without the human nature contaminating the Divinity.

The sick room is close, and the air is full of fever-poison. Throw open the window, and the sweet pure air of heaven puffs in and banishes all the poison from that stifling air, removes the closeness, sweetens the room. Human nature is that fever-haunted atmosphere, CHRIST is the open window through Whom Divine holiness wafts into mankind to purify. But the pestilential atmosphere does not poison heaven's breezes.

Dark is the dungeon. No ray of heaven penetrates, but only a sickly glimmer. The walls are covered with slimy fungus-growth, foul creatures that love darkness rustle in the straw, and race over the floor. Suddenly the door is thrown open, and the golden sun and the blue sky shine into that hideous dungeon, drying the damp walls, dispelling the darkness, routing the noisome vermin who love it. Mankind was that dark cell, CHRIST is the open door, through which the Godhead shines in to enlighten. But the darkness does not dusk the daylight.

It is through the channel alone that the renovating flood enters the pool.

It is through the window alone that the purifying air blows into the room.

It is through the door alone that the illumining beam penetrates the dungeon.

It is through CHRIST alone that Grace is given to man to renovate, to purify, to enlighten. And Grace is a portion of the Divine Nature.

The old covenant with the Jews was one of forbidding only. The new covenant is one of Grace helping also. Under the old law men were ordered not to do this, and not to do that; in one word GOD told them what things they must avoid, if they were to save themselves from ruin of all their happiness. Under the new law men are given help, they are made partakers of the nature of GOD, to enable them to keep the law of GOD, not in the letter only, but in the spirit also.

The Jew did his best unaided; the Christian does his best, CHRIST helping him.

How it is that Grace is given and we are made partakers of the Divine Nature, I shall tell you on another occasion.

X.

CHRIST THE EXAMPLE.

" I have given you an example, that ye should do as I have done to you."—S. John xiii. 15.

IN a former sermon I showed you how our LORD JESUS CHRIST came to teach the Truth to men.

I intend to-day to show you how He also sets men an example of following that heavenly doctrine He taught.

There is a very homely and true proverb, that "Example is better than precept." Take a book teaching joiners' art, and try to become a carpenter from the rules given in that book. A sorry carpenter you will prove. But go and watch a joiner at his work, and see how he carries out all the rules contained in the book, and you will be able to follow them also.

Or go to sea in charge of a large vessel, having only acquired your knowledge of managing ships from what an old sea-captain has told you, and you will wreck the boat. But if you go several cruises with the captain and watch how he manages, see how he reads the chart and steers the vessel, and manages her in a heavy sea,—why then, in time, you will be able to do the same.

Now suppose we had only CHRIST'S teaching, only what He told us was the will of GOD, then there might arise some misunderstanding of His meaning, or men might say that GOD has declared to us a law which it is impossible for us to fulfil.

In order, then, to show us how to obey the will of GOD,

and how to keep His law, CHRIST took human nature upon Him with all its infirmities, and lived among men a life in strict accordance with the law which He taught men.

This is not all. There are really three laws given to men. There is first the *Natural law*. That is what we get by the light of nature. Most people, whatever their religion, have got some notions in their heads that society cannot get on if murder, adultery, theft, and slander are allowed. And they think that, if there is a GOD, He certainly expects some sort of worship. This is called the Natural law, or the law which people's common sense would point out to them as right, if they give their minds to it.

Then, secondly, there is the *Jewish law*. This commanded certain rites and ceremonies to the Jewish people. All such rites and ceremonies pointed to CHRIST to fulfil them and give them a meaning which they had not in themselves. The Jews had also the natural law written with the finger of GOD for them, very plainly, in the Ten Commandments.

Then thirdly there is the *Christian law*. This commands that we should observe the commands of the natural law not in the letter only, but in the spirit also. The natural law forbade murder. The Christian law strikes at the root of the evil, and forbids bearing hatred and malice in the heart, which is the temper which, if given way to, leads to murder. The natural law forbids adultery. The Christian law not only forbids a man taking to him another man's wife, but it forbids all acts of uncleanness, and it forbids a man harbouring wishes that are not seemly in his innermost heart.

The natural law forbids theft. The Christian law forbids any one wishing to have that which belongs to another, and envying and grudging him the possession of it.

The natural law required man to perform certain outward acts of worship to GOD. The Christian law bids him not only perform these acts outwardly, but do them with a reverent spirit, and give Him the homage of the heart and mind as well.

Our LORD JESUS CHRIST, to set all men an example, fulfilled all three laws. He observed the natural law, avoiding all open sin. He kept the Jewish law, observing all the ceremonies ordained by Moses. And at His Baptism with the descent of the HOLY GHOST, He passed under the Christian law, or the dispensation of Grace, to show men how man, assisted by Grace, can keep the Christian law, and observe the Ten Commandments in the spirit as well as in the letter.

Thus the heathen can look to CHRIST, and see Him perfectly keeping that natural law which he lives under. The Jew can look to CHRIST, and see Him fulfilling the graceless formalities of the Old Covenant. The Christian can look to CHRIST, and see a perfect example under that spiritual law which He Himself revealed to men.

Now look what a different sort of perfection is set us by these three laws. Under the natural law a man is an excellent fellow, a model of virtue, if he is strict in his worship of GOD, his regard for his parents; and is not a murderer, an adulterer, a thief, a slanderer, and an avaricious man. Under the Jewish law, a man was a great and holy man if, in addition to the natural law, he was strict in his fasts, offered his sacrifices with regularity, and was rigid in his observance of the Sabbath.

But the Christian idea is far higher. It is the highest possible type of perfection. "Be ye therefore perfect, even as My FATHER which is in heaven is perfect." That was the goal CHRIST set before us,—never to rest content till we are like GOD.

And then, to help us He set us an example. In everything He was without blame, holy, harmless, undefiled.

It is remarkable that there is scarcely a perfect character in the Old Testament. We do not know of any one who perfectly kept the Old Law. Some of the greatest of the Old Testament characters were guilty of grievous sins, or weaknesses. They were best before the law was given by Moses; then they walked by the law of nature, or common-sense. But when the Law came " sin revived and they died." Moses showed anger and presumption, Samson betrayed the LORD's secret, David was guilty of adultery and murder, Solomon of idolatry, Hezekiah of vain-glory, Jotham of weakness—" The high places were not taken away,"—Josiah of presumption, in fighting Necho, when GOD had not ordered him.

But CHRIST's example is without flaw. " He did no sin, neither was guile found in His lips."

If a child seeks a model, he finds it in JESUS subject to His parents, working in Nazareth, leading a hidden life, not forward, noisy, pushing, but bashful and submissive. Loving instruction, moreover, seeking the temple, listening to wise teachers, and throughout penetrated with the sense of obligation to do the FATHER's business, to keep GOD's will.

If the adult seeks a pattern, he finds it in the Man JESUS, diligent, resisting the Devil, eschewing vain ambition, controlling the flesh by fasting, elevating the spirit by prayer, patient, self-contained, courteous, generous, upright, pure, humble, but without loss of self-respect.

Does the priest seek a pattern? He finds one in the great High Priest JESUS, going about seeking and saving those that were lost, tender to the fallen, gentle in reproof of sinners, but steadfast against sin.

Does the tempted seek a pattern how he may resist? He finds it in JESUS in the wilderness. Hence he draws his lesson with what weapons, and in what manner he is to fight the tempter.

Does the bereaved seek a pattern how he may bear his loss? He finds it in JESUS at the tomb of Lazarus, weeping, but full of confidence in the resurrection, full of sweet trust that death is a sleep from which there is a glad awaking.

Does the deserted seek a pattern how he may bear his agony? He finds it in JESUS deserted by His disciples, betrayed by one apostle, denied by another. Not angry, returning the kiss of the betrayer, turning with a loving look on the denier, loving still, and ready to forgive all who deserted Him.

Does the lonely one seek a pattern how he may bear his isolation? He finds it in JESUS, alone on the mountain-top in meditation, alone in the garden praying in an agony, with an angel comforting Him, alone on the Cross, His Mother and the other women standing afar off, patient, hoping, conscious of the ever-abiding presence of GOD.

Does the sufferer in bodily pain seek a pattern? He looks to JESUS, scourged, bruised, nailed to the tree, and finds Him not thinking of self, but of others. "FATHER, forgive them, for they know not what they do!" Considerate of His fellow-sufferer, "This day shalt thou be with Me in Paradise." And of His relations, "Behold thy mother;" "Woman, behold thy son." Patient and unrepining.

Does the dying seek a pattern? He sees it in JESUS commending His Spirit into the hands of the FATHER, and withdrawing His head from honours of the world, the vain title written above on the Cross, when He bowed His head and gave up the ghost.

Thus, my brethren, we find in everything that CHRIST is our pattern, our great Example, by Whom we must rule our lives. To unfold to us His life to be our pattern, the four Gospels were written. In them we look, and we see as in a mirror our own shortcomings. We measure ourselves by that perfect example, and learn how to amend. We press forward to the mark of our high calling, ever looking unto JESUS the author and finisher of our faith.

Have you ever seen printers at work? They set up the copy before them, and then they reproduce it with the type at their disposal. Then they carefully go over what they have set up, and revise it by the copy. Here there is a wrong letter, there there is a letter turned upside down. With their eye on the copy they pluck out the wrong character, and set in its place the right one, or they reverse the inverted letter. Now when the printer has done, what he has set up is gone over at least twice; once, what is called the proof is examined, then the revise is gone over, and the mistakes are marked, and he corrects his block of type again and again.

So should it be with us. Before us, in the Holy Gospels, is set up the perfect copy, the pattern of JESUS CHRIST, which we have to reproduce in ourselves. S. Paul speaks of CHRIST being formed in us. It is by self-examination that we prove and revise our lives. We look at the Sermon on the Mount, and the example of CHRIST, and then we look at our own acts and words and thoughts, and see if they are in any way unlike CHRIST and inconsistent with His teaching. If so, we pull the evil out by an act of contrition

and confession, and try to model ourselves more into con-
formity with the law and life of CHRIST. By degrees our
eyes get accustomed to see inaccuracies, and detect errors
which at first we passed over, not noticing them ; and thus
by practice and self-examination, and watchfulness, we are
able more and more to approach to the likeness of CHRIST,
to attain to the measure of the stature of the fulness of
CHRIST, and to near that perfection which is to be the aim
of our whole lives.

XI.

THE INCARNATION.

" We walk by faith, not by sight."—2 Cor. v. 7.

OUR LORD JESUS CHRIST is GOD and Man. The nature
of GOD and the nature of man are in Him indissolubly
united. In this statement you have the foundation of
Christianity.

Now let us see what we mean by this.

We mean that JESUS CHRIST is GOD ; and as GOD is
eternal, that there never was a time when He was not, there
never will be a time when He will not be.

As GOD He is also everywhere present. There is no
place in heaven or earth where GOD is not.

But we believe also, that as Man there was a time when
He was born, a time when He died ; He was in one place
and not in another, in the crib of Bethlehem, in the work-
shop of Nazareth, by the lake side preaching, in Gethsemane
praying, on Calvary dying.

Here, you may say, is a contradiction. But though it may appear so, it is not a real contradiction. He was not born as GOD, but as man, He did not die as GOD, but as man. It was not the Godhead which was brought into existence from Mary's womb; the Godhead was not wounded by the nails and the spear.

As JESUS CHRIST walked on earth, men looked on Him, and with their senses perceived only the Manhood, but with the spiritual part of their being became dimly conscious of the Godhead. In CHRIST there was the Manhood which men could see, touch, hear; and there was the Godhead which they could not see, touch, and hear.

And these two natures were closely united, as the soul and body are united in one man. I can see you, I can touch you, I can hear you; but I cannot see, touch, and hear your soul. Now JESUS CHRIST took a man's soul on Him in addition to a man's body; and the Godhead in Him was as closely united to the human body and soul, as the human soul in you is united to your human body. Your finger may be cut off, but it does not make your soul smaller; your arm may be amputated, but it does not weaken your soul; your head may be cut off, but it does not kill your soul;—so the body of JESUS CHRIST might be hurt, and wounded, and slain, but His Godhead remained impassible, that is, could not be hurt, wounded, or slain.

Again, a man's soul without a body, how can it communicate with man? It may love, think, wish, hope, but it cannot express itself so as to make you conscious. A man's soul can communicate with spiritual beings, but it cannot with human beings unless it has a body. The soul uses the body to communicate with men. It makes the tongue speak its ideas, and the hand execute its wishes. Cut out

F

my tongue and amputate my hand, and my soul is helpless
in conveying its ideas to you. I can make you hear and
understand what is passing in my soul, because I have a
tongue. If I lose my tongue, my soul is just as active, but
it cannot communicate its activity to you.

So GOD to communicate with man, to convey His thoughts
and wishes to man, took on Him a man's body, that He
might speak to man with a human voice, and act the thoughts
of GOD, with human limbs, hands, and feet.

The Incarnation—that is what the flesh-taking of the SON
of GOD is called—was the revealing to man of the love and
will of GOD.

Now all creation is, in some sort, an incarnation of the
thoughts of GOD, to make them understandable by man. If
it were not for the world and all the things GOD has made
in it, we should have no idea as to what the thoughts of
GOD were. Look, as you go home, at the sun gleaming on
the blue sea, look at the green elms on the hedge banks,
look at the germander speedwells by the road side, and the
great bunch of mallows by the spring. All these beautiful
things are GOD's ideas made visible to us. The ideas of the
sea and the sun were in His mind, and these ideas took
shape by His creating word, and so we know what were the
thoughts of GOD, by the things of GOD we see. We know
by looking at the speedwell and the mallow what were the
thoughts of GOD just as we know by the words of a letter
what the person was thinking when he wrote it, just as we
know by a painting what were the beautiful ideas of the
artist. The works of creation are the thoughts of GOD
articulated so as to impress men's senses.

But the Incarnation of the SON of GOD is more than this.
It is GOD the SON, Himself, becoming man to impress the

thoughts and purposes of GOD not on man's senses only, but through his senses on his moral nature.

Very well, then, my brethren, JESUS CHRIST is GOD and man. As GOD invisible, inward and spiritual; as man visible, outward and material.

Then all His relations with man will partake of His nature. That is in all His dealings with us, there will be a part invisible and spiritual, and a part visible and material.

For what purpose did CHRIST come on earth?

To teach and to help. To teach men how to become perfectly happy, and to help men to accomplish that which will alone make them perfectly happy.

Therefore in His teaching and in His helping, we shall expect to find an outward, visible part, and also an inward spiritual part. An outward part that will correspond with His manhood, an inward part that will correspond with His Godhead. A material part that will be like the body of man; a spiritual part that will be like the soul of man.

Now the teaching of the Truth was committed by CHRIST to His Church, when He said, "Go ye into all the world, and preach the Gospel to every creature, ... and lo, I am with you always even unto the end of the world." Thus the Church is the teaching body. It is a visible Church, commissioned by CHRIST to teach the truth, and the teaching body is the clergy,—the bishops, priests, and deacons. The Church is an organized body ever preserving the truth, and with the promise given to it of infallibility, that is of never, as a whole, falling into error. Therefore if we find that the .Church everywhere, and in all ages, has taught certain doctrines, those doctrines we may be perfectly sure are true.

Then again the Bible contains the teaching of CHRIST.

In the early ages of the Church, there were a great number of Gospels and Epistles used. Then the Church, by virtue of her authority as the teaching body, chose which Gospels and which Epistles should be bound up together in one volume, and should be used for the edification of the faithful, and rejected those she regarded as false, or allowed men to read the other as useful, but not to be received on the same high grounds, because she did not authorize all that was contained in them as true.

Now when we take these Bibles, what have we got?

The outward and visible form, the letter-press and paper, and the inward and spiritual part, the Divine Truth.

We cannot arrive at the Truth without the Bible and the Church, that is, without the outward forms. Nor would the mere book, and the mere organized body of the Church, be of any use to us unless there were the inward and spiritual part, the Divine authority teaching the Truth.

But now that CHRIST has come, and is the head over all things, we cannot have the spirit without the letter, and the form without the truth. The two are so bound up together as to be inseparable. "What GOD has joined together, let not man put asunder."

Then again with regard to Grace. We shall find that Grace is always given in accordance with the law of the Incarnation. I mean, that where GOD gives Divine help, He gives it through outward and visible means.

GOD gives Grace through the Sacraments. The Sacraments are the means whereby GOD communicates to us strength to keep His law and believe His truth.

In the Grace-giving of GOD there must be a part answering to the manhood of CHRIST, and a part answering to the Godhead of CHRIST; a part corresponding to the body of man, and a part corresponding to the soul of man. And this we find is the fact.

In the Sacraments there is always something visible and outward, but there is, also, always something invisible and inward. Every Sacrament has a soul.

Now let us look at Baptism. There is an outward form, water poured on the child and certain words uttered. But that is not all. If we regard Baptism as an outward form only we make as great a mistake as if we treat all men as soulless creatures, mere walking bodies.

No, in Baptism there is an inward and spiritual grace, a death unto original sin, a new birth unto righteousness, a giving of Grace, of GOD the HOLY GHOST, to enable the child to lead a godly Christian life, if it chooses.

Then in Confirmation, there is an outward form, the laying on of the bishop's hands, and the invocation of the HOLY GHOST. But that is not all. There is a soul in Confirmation as well as a body. The inward spiritual part is a descent of GOD the HOLY GHOST to strengthen.

So in the Holy Eucharist. What we see and touch and taste is bread and wine, over which the consecrating words are said ; but they cease from that moment to be mere outward and visible signs. They are now Grace-giving ; the Body and Blood of CHRIST to be our spiritual food and nourishment.

I might speak also of Penance and Ordination. In both there is the outward part, in both the inward spiritual grace-giving ; but you can follow these out for yourselves.

The Sacramental act is the joining on of the outward form to CHRIST, Who is both outward and visible and also inward and spiritual, and this joining on to Him at once sends Grace flowing through it to the recipient. Let me give you an illustration or two. You may have seen how the electric telegraph is worked. There is a great battery which pours electricity through the wires. Now if there are no wires leading from London to Colchester, the battery then will send no telegrams to Colchester. But the moment the wires are placed in conjunction with the battery, the message is shot through them instantaneously to its destination.

The battery is CHRIST, the electricity is Grace, the wires are the outward forms of the Sacrament.

A fountain pours forth abundance of water. A mile off is the village with no fountain in it. Pipes are laid down all along to the village. The pipes themselves are dry and give no water. But the moment the last pipe is applied to the spring, the stream shoots along them, and pours its flood into the thirsty village.

CHRIST is the fountain, Grace is the water, the pipes are the Sacraments.

You know how common it is for people to despise and run down the Sacraments, and call them empty forms. That is because they do not understand the main principle of Christianity. They are not real Christians. The main principle of Christianity is,—Outward forms the channels of Grace. Under the Jewish dispensation there were forms only. Under the Christian dispensation all the forms flow with Grace. That is what S. Paul means when he says that we walk by faith and not by sight. To the sight, the Sacraments are only forms, to faith they are channels of Grace. To sight Baptism is only a ceremony, to faith it is a regeneration. To sight Holy Communion is only bread and wine, to faith it is the Body and Blood of CHRIST.

Many years ago my father went for the winter into a town, and we took with us our country servants. We hired a house in which gas was laid down. Now the servants had never seen gas used before, for at that time it was not so common as now.

When they were told to light the gas, the servants laughed. "Who ever heard of putting a match to an iron bar! How could an iron bar do any good?" "If I was master," said the cook, "I would tear up all these iron things and throw them out of the house, worthless things that they are!"

Too many people regard Sacraments as those servants regarded the gas-pipes, because they cannot *see* Grace, they do not believe it is present.

A few years ago some workmen were ordered to bury a lot of nitro-glycerine in a field out of harm's way. They dug a large pit, and threw in the nitro-glycerine. "I cannot think," said one of the men, "why people can make such a fuss about this. There's nothing to be afraid of in it. Why, look here! it is just like sugar-candy, see!" And lifting his spade he struck the crystals, and was blown with several of his companions into eternity.

Too many people regard the Sacraments as that man regarded the nitro-glycerine, and approach them carelessly, disbelieving in their awful power, because they are to the *sight* only material forms.

XII.

GRACE AND FREE WILL.

"Seek, and ye shall find."—S. Matth. vii. 7.

FROM this pulpit, I can see through the window a ship, a collier, if I am not mistaken, bound for Maldon. She has come from Newcastle, all her sails are spread, the wind is favourable, and she is cutting through the water, and will soon have doubled the point and entered the Blackwater.

If the wind blows, and the ship's sails are not spread, she will not advance on her course; she will not reach her destination.

If the ship's sails be spread and no wind blows, she will lie becalmed, and cannot continue her course. There she will lie, her sails drooping, her hull motionless.

It is of no use the wind blowing unless her sails be spread; it is of no use spreading the sails unless the wind blows.

Grace is the breeze, man's will is the sail.

Man is bound for the port of heaven, GOD's grace will not carry him there, unless he wills to go along with Grace. Man may will to reach heaven, but without grace he cannot get there. He lies becalmed.

Now some people make great blunders about this. Some say, Oh! we can do what is right without grace. We have hearty, strong wills of our own, and if we choose we can lead decent Christian lives without GOD's help. That is heresy. Heresy means an error in religious truth. To suppose that we can do all that is required of us by GOD, that we can reach heaven by our own might, and the force of our own resolutions, is to suppose wrong. Those who think so are heretics; that is, they have made a blunder about the Truth.

This is shocking to hear stated broadly. We think,—How impious those men must be who suppose that they are sufficient of themselves to do what is right, and to go on their heavenward course, and reach the promised haven, without GOD's help. We never heard of such people! Do you think so? Well, I have seen plenty of them. And if I am not much mistaken, we have rather too many of them in this parish. I do not mean to say that they say right out "We can do very well without GOD's grace," but they act precisely as if they could do without it. They go on from year to year without seeking it. They lie always off the same point of land, not because the breeze of grace is not blowing, but because they will not spread their sails to catch it. ·

You will see that I am not wrong when you consider how Grace is given to men.

How, then, is grace given? Why, my brethren, through the Sacraments. They are the means of grace provided by GOD to supply us with the strength we need to carry us on our course, to make us fight the good fight of faith, to lay hold of Eternal Life. How many of you take in a supply of grace? How many of you kneel about that Altar and seek and get GOD's help to enable you to go on your course, not in your own might, but with the grace of GOD helping your infirmities?

You know the spring of clear water close by the churchyard: and you know S. Peter's well at West Mersea, always full and overflowing. You know also that in dry

summers, people come from every part of the parish to this
our church spring to get water, and that people send from
miles round to S. Peter's well for water, from Langerhoe
and Abberton and Great Wigborough and Peldon. What
should you think of people dying of thirst, whilst these
wells flow over all the year through, because they will not
take the trouble of sending to them for water? What
should you think of people trying to live without water
altogether, because it is so far to send for pure spring
water?

Why! my brethren, here are the Wells of Salvation!
Here in this font, there on that altar, the fountains of grace
flow, flow, flow all through the year, pouring out grace
abundantly, grace to heal each deadly· wound, grace to
strengthen the weak, grace to fortify the timorous, grace
to cheer the sad, grace to guide the doubting, grace to
cleanse the stained.

Why remain weak, when strength is to be found here?
Why continue feeble of heart, when spiritual might is given
here? Why remain sad, when here grace flows to cheer?
Why be longer in doubt, when counsel is dispensed here?
Why continue soiled with sin, when here the cleansing flood
is poured forth?

Why?—why because you act as if you thought that you
could reach heaven without GOD'S grace. You can't; and
you will find out your mistake too late.

But now let us see what the other blunder in religious
truth is, into which men sometimes fall. They say: Oh!
the grace of GOD is all-powerful; when GOD wills, He will
waft me on. Grace will do all for me. I have nothing
to do myself, except to accept free salvation. This means
that we.are to sit with our hands on our laps, and let GOD

do everything for us! That we are to let the grace of God waft us on, without spreading sail or touching the rudder!

That is a most dangerous heresy, or false belief. It tends to make men indifferent to God's law, to inflate them with false confidence and spiritual pride.

It never will do for men to take hold of one truth and run it to extremes, and neglect the other truth which corrects the former, and balances it.

The world you know swings round the sun. The sun has, so to speak, a strong pull on the earth. But if there were no other force to keep this pull of the sun in check, the sun would drag the earth down on itself and burn us all up. But this pull of the sun is controlled by a force in the revolving earth which tends to make it fly away through the vast, dark, infinite sky. If it were not for the pull of the sun on the earth, we should be whirled away into awful darkness and fierce cold, which would freeze us all as hard as iron. So you see our safety and our well-being lies in these two forces just balancing one another. Thus is it in the domain of religious truths. Our Christian Faith is full of truths which are holding each other in check, and correcting one another. If we take hold of one, and deny the other, we are in error, and make dreadful mistakes. It is so in what I am explaining to you now—the relation between the Grace of God and the Free Will of man.

If we think the grace of God so powerful that it forces men to salvation without their co-operation,—we are in error.

If, on the other hand, we think the will of man so strong that he can do all necessary to salvation,—then we are in error again.

"Stir up, we beseech Thee, O Lord, the wills of Thy

faithful people." So begins the Collect for the Last Sunday after Trinity. In it we ask GOD to send His quickening breath to awaken in us our sleeping will. Just as the sailors, when they feel the fanning of the gentle breeze, and see it curling the waves, at once start from their lethargy, and run to the ropes and hoist the sails; so we must first feel the soft breathing of Divine grace stir our hearts, before we put forth our will to enable us to catch the wind that will bear us. forward. As the warm air and genial sun in the spring must first soften and heat the clods before the seeds swell and thrust up the stalks and leaves, so must the grace of GOD first stir up the hearts of GOD's faithful people, that they may strive to bring forth plenteously the fruits of good works which will of GOD be plenteously rewarded.

Next, then, comes the striving of man to correspond to grace, as it is called, that is, to do all that GOD has commanded, so that grace may be able to act freely and fully on him, to advance him in his spiritual course.

At our Baptism we were placed in GOD's service. We undertook to believe certain truths, and to keep certain laws. Now without GOD's grace we cannot do either. GOD must inspire us with faith to believe the truths of Revelation, and GOD must enable us to keep His laws. We can do neither without His help. I do not mean to say that a man might not tacitly acquiesce in the revealed truth, and keep the letter of the law, by his unaided efforts; but without the grace of GOD inspiring him he cannot have a lively faith. The Articles of the Creed may be sown in his heart, but they are dead till the soft spring breath of GOD blows and quickens them into living springs of action. So with the Commandments. They are to be observed in the spirit as well as in the letter; and to observe them in the spirit, which is demanded of Christians, is quite impossible for any man unassisted by grace.

Well, my brethren, you have engaged at your baptism heartily to believe the truth, and heartily to keep the law of GOD. To do this, you must have the grace of GOD. And GOD only gives His grace if He sees you ready to use your utmost endeavours to make grace effectual.

If GOD gives you light, He expects you to open your eyes and look about you. If GOD gives you air to breathe, He expects that you will give your lungs play. If you put a bandage over your mouth and nose, the air won't enter your lungs and force you to live. So if GOD gives His grace to enable us to lead Christian lives, He requires us to do all we can to enable grace to work out life to our souls within us. We are not dead logs to be blown about and drift before grace; but we are living plants growing through the assistance of grace; but having an independent active corresponding will within us.

And in conclusion, think of this. If we put forth our wills and try to serve GOD, and make use of grace given to enable us to serve GOD, then GOD in the end rewards us, just as if we had done all by ourselves unaided; "Well done, good and faithful servant, enter thou into the joy of thy LORD."

"Stir up, we beseech Thee, O LORD, the wills of Thy faithful people, that they plenteously bringing forth the fruit of good works, may of Thee be plenteously rewarded; through JESUS CHRIST our LORD. Amen."

XIII.

THE ATONEMENT.

"Christ also hath once suffered for sins, the Just for the unjust, that He might bring us to God."—1 S. Pet. iii. 18.

SIN brings in its train two consequences, *guilt*, and *suffering*. By sin we become guilty in the sight of GOD, and we suffer in ourselves.

CHRIST died for our sins. That is, He died to take away all the guilt of our sins, and so to reconcile us to GOD. But He does not, by His death, wholly remove the suffering consequent on sin.

For instance. A man by an act of drunkenness becomes guilty before GOD, and brings on himself violent headache. He may bitterly repent and be pardoned through CHRIST. But that does not remove his headache. A man may ruin his constitution by a life of debauchery, and turn in bitter contrition to the Cross of CHRIST, and find pardon; but that does not restore to him his lost vigour of constitution. Now CHRIST suffered great pains on the Cross, not for His sins, for He was sinless, and since then many of His servants have suffered; thus from age to age continuing to "fill up what is behind of the sufferings of CHRIST" (Col. i. 24), so that there is an abundant treasure from which CHRIST may take to apply for the assuaging of the pain.

But it is not of this I am going to speak now.

I am going on this occasion to direct your attention to the Sacrifice of the death of CHRIST as removing our *guilt*.

Sin is abhorrent to GOD. He cannot endure it. For

Him to be reconciled with man, it must be removed. Till it is taken away He cannot fill the soul with spiritual things, just as the sun cannot shine into the room, the windows of which are smeared over with lamp-black.

In my father's garden is a fountain, which used to throw up its water high into the air. But by degrees the water became lower, and at last ceased to flow altogether. My father had the pipes examined, and he found that an ash tree had thrust a little thread of root in at a junction of the pipes, the fibre had grown, and thrown out a network of other fibres, and these in turn had spread and thrown out others, till in time the pipe was choked as completely as if with a mass of felt. When this was cleared out, the fountain played as before.

Now it is very evident that men could not cleanse their own consciences from dead works,—that is, sins,—to serve the living GOD. Some one else must do that. CHRIST came to give grace, but in order that grace may flow, He must also remove the choking root of sin.

For this purpose He died.

It is very true that CHRIST, by His voluntary submission to the will of the FATHER, in taking human flesh upon Him, merited the remission of the sins of the whole world. By any one act He might have satisfied the FATHER, and obtained the reconciliation of the world, but He willed that His obedience should be perfect, that man should not be redeemed but by suffering to Himself, as a proof to man of the heinousness of sin, and of His own wondrous love. He was resolved also, inasmuch as He took man's nature upon Him, that He would take it with all it is called on to endure; that He might suffer in His friends who forsook Him; in His reputation, by the blasphemous accusations of His enemies; in His honour and self-respect, by the mockeries of the soldiers; in His substance, by His poverty, and the spoiling of His vesture; in His soul, by sadness, weariness, and fear; in His body, by wounds and stripes. He suffered in the members of His body, in His head, pierced by the crown of thorns; in His hands and feet, riven by the nails; in His face, by the smitings and spittings; in His whole body, by the scourgings; in His heart, by the soldier's spear that transfixed it. He suffered in every bodily sense;—in touch, by the scourgings and nails; in taste, by the vinegar and gall; in smell, by the loathsome odours of that charnel, Golgotha; in hearing, by the blasphemies and mockings; and in sight, by the tears of Mary and the disciple whom He loved.

CHRIST's death was a full, perfect, and sufficient sacrifice for sin. Just as, by disobedience, misery came into the world, so by obedience comes the restoration from misery. Adam set his will against the will of GOD. CHRIST set His human will in agreement with the will of GOD. And as the sin of Adam brought pain and death on all his children and their descendants, so the obedience of CHRIST restores to health and happiness all such as are united to Him, and became His sons by adoption and grace.

We call CHRIST's death an *Atonement*, because thereby He has made at-one those who were separated,—GOD and man. The sin of man stood as a barrier between them. CHRIST came and removed the barrier, and with the removal made man and GOD once more at-one.

We also call CHRIST's death our *Redemption*. To redeem means to buy back out of slavery those who once were free. In olden times pirates used to cruise about our shores, and carry off men and children to Barbary, where they sold them as slaves. Slaves cannot free themselves, for all their work is for their master, not for themselves; they cannot earn money, for their time and their earnings are not their own, but belong to their master.

In those days good men used to go out to Barbary with a large sum of money, and pay down the price of a slave, and set him free. Then the redeemed man returned in the ship to his own dear home; of course, if he chose, he might run back to the service of the slave-driver; but in all probability he would thankfully return whence he had been taken, to home and to freedom.

Now man was free in Eden, GOD made him to be free and happy. But Adam by his fault lost his freedom, and became a slave to sin, bound with the fetters of bad habits; and a slave's children born in slavery are slaves also, so the children of Adam born in sin, continue in the bondage of evil.

CHRIST came to set man free; He paid the price of His all-prevailing merits, His perfect obedience unto death, His most precious Blood, and so redeemed man, brought him out of bondage, and set him in the glorious liberty of the children of GOD. Baptism is the application of the merits of CHRIST for the purchase of the child, to bring it into freedom.

A redeemed person may, if he chooses, fall back into the bondage of sin; redemption does not necessarily save him; he must co-operate with grace, use his own free-will, and do his best, if he is to reach his own dear home, Paradise. But unless the price is paid down, and he is redeemed, all his attempts are in vain. And this is what the article means when it says that works done before Justification are not availing.

G

Then, again, CHRIST died to make *satisfaction*, for sin. That means, to satisfy the righteousness, or justice of GOD. He by His obedience and death is able to reconcile the mercy with the justice of GOD. GOD's law is that suffering and death should be the consequence of sin, and that unremitted sin should cause endless suffering and eternal death. With GOD, and in His service, is perfect happiness, and eternal life. Separation from Him, through disobedience, is misery and death. Consequently to unite us again to Him is to restore us to happiness, but that happiness can only continue as long as we live according to His will.

CHRIST, by His sufferings and death, satisfies the law of GOD, and then He brings men back into union with GOD and life, their disobedience and sin that is past being pardoned for the sake of the sufferings of CHRIST.

Therefore you see that all our hope and trust must be in the Cross of CHRIST, for thereby we obtain remission of our sins, we satisfy the justice of GOD, GOD is reconciled with sinners, and we are brought out of bondage into liberty.

And the death of CHRIST is calculated to teach us the awful wickedness of sin, how loathsome it is in GOD's sight, how it cuts off from grace, how it obscures the light of His countenance, and brings us into misery.

It is calculated also to show us how great is the love of CHRIST for us, that He came seeking man's affection wherever He might find it, even in the pangs of death.

"If I be lifted up from the earth, I will draw all men unto Me," said our Blessed LORD; and true indeed has been that saying. JESUS crucified has melted the hardest hearts, JESUS crucified has attracted the warmest love, JESUS crucified has been the trust of the living, and the confidence of the dying.

XIV.

THE SACRIFICE.

"As often as ye eat this bread and drink this cup, ye do show the Lord's death till He come."—1 Cor. xi. 26.

OUR LORD died on the cross more than eighteen hundred years ago. He died as a sacrifice for sin, to remove that sin which prevented man from receiving grace, and which separated him from the FATHER.

Now you cannot take away that which does not exist. You cannot take a book off a table when no book is on the table. So sin cannot be taken away, when the sin has not been committed, and will not be for over a thousand years.

If sin is being continually committed, a continual sacrifice for sin is needed, so as to take it away, when it does exist. If slavery were to be introduced into England a hundred years hence, the ill results of such a course cannot be obviated now, and the law allowing it cannot be repealed till slavery in England is a fact. So sin cannot be repealed, sacrifice for sin cannot remove it, till the sin is a fact. And it is evident that we who live more than eighteen hundred years after CHRIST need a sacrifice for sin, quite as much as did men at the time when CHRIST died. Our souls are just as precious as theirs.

But then, we know that CHRIST died only once, and that He cannot come down and die for sin year after year. "CHRIST," says S. Peter, "hath once suffered for sins, the just for the unjust." (1 S. Pet. iii. 18.) "Now once in the end of the world hath He appeared to put away sin by the sacrifice of Himself. And as it is appointed unto men once to die, but after this the judgment: So CHRIST was once offered to bear the sins of many; and unto them that look for Him shall He appear the second time without sin unto salvation." (Heb. ix. 26—28.)

So far then is clear, that CHRIST dieth no more. The scene of Calvary is over for ever. There is no more suffering for the holy JESUS. The blood-shedding for the remission of sins is a thing of the past.

But at the same time it is necessary for us that, as we sin, we should have a sacrifice to offer to the FATHER to be a propitiation for our sins. And also it is clear that no other sacrifice will avail, except the sacrifice of CHRIST, for none other can remit guilt.

How then is this difficulty solved? By the perpetuation of the sacrifice *without* the suffering and the blood-shedding. The sacrifice, as to pain and death is over, the sacrifice as to remission of sin will not cease till sin is no more.

Now CHRIST Himself provided a way whereby the sacrifice of His death should be perpetuated till His second coming. The last night before His death He took bread and brake, and gave to His disciples, and said, "This is My Body;" He took the cup and blessed, and gave it to them, and said, "This is My Blood;" and He added, "this do in remembrance of Me." Now the word remembrance as it is in the original language in which the Gospel is written, does not mean what we do by the word "remembrance," but means a memorial, a reminder to some one else. So that our LORD's words really mean, "Do this as a memorial or reminder of Me." And to whom should this memorial be made, but to GOD the FATHER? As often as men sin, and incur GOD's wrath, let them do this, offer this reminder to the FATHER of the merits of the death of CHRIST, and looking on the face of His Anointed, for His sake, He will pardon the offence.

The holy Eucharist then is the Sacrifice of the Death of CHRIST, which we show forth to GOD the FATHER. Now we generally call that blessed Sacrament "the Holy Communion," and we mean that in it GOD gives to us the Body and Blood of CHRIST. But we must not forget that this is a very inadequate name to express this Sacrament, for not only in it do we *get* something, but in it we *give* something. We are too eager to be always getting to think much of giving. Yet unless we give, we cannot get. That is, unless we offer to GOD the Sacrifice to obtain pardon for our sins, and so to remove them, our sins remain and obstruct the flow of grace, so that we cannot get all we need.

In the holy Sacrifice of the Altar we plead the death of CHRIST with the FATHER, we show His wounds, His blood, to the FATHER, and as the merits of CHRIST are perfect, GOD for CHRIST'S sake pardons us. But if we approach GOD without pleading CHRIST'S merits, we are rushing boldly to the throne of grace with all our sins clinging to us, in a condition utterly unfit to receive grace beneficially.

Now some people, who know no better,—poor things!— say, "what is the good of being present at Holy Communion when you do not communicate?" We are not always sufficiently prepared to receive the highest and most awful gift GOD can give to man ; but we can always plead the death of CHRIST in expiation of our sins, and ask to be made more worthy through the merits of CHRIST'S Passion.

The distinguishing feature of the Christian religion is, that it does not admit of vagueness, but brings everything to a point, a *when*, and a *where*. Before CHRIST came, people

thought GOD was everywhere, and some considered that
therefore there was no particular place or time for worship
and prayer, and so what is no particular place soon came to
be nowhere, and what is no particular time soon came to be
never.   But when CHRIST was on earth—there He was on
one particular spot.   He was in one place one day, He was
in another place next day.   If a leper wanted to be healed,
it would not do for him to sit quietly at home, and say,
"CHRIST is GOD, He is everywhere present, therefore I need
not go at such an hour to such a place to find Him and be
healed."   No ! if the leper went ten minutes too late, or
half a mile out of his road, he missed CHRIST JESUS, and
remained in his leprosy.

And this characterizes the whole Christian religion.   It
is a religion of time and place, though not exclusively.
That is to say, we can pray to GOD at any time and everywhere ; but for the special purposes for which CHRIST came
on earth, there are fixed times, and fixed places, and fixed
ways, in which He is present, and acts, and dispenses grace.

Now in the matter of the holy Sacrament it is so.   That
is the way, *the* way, in which He requires His Sacrifice to
be offered and perpetuated to the end of the world.   If we
are present and plead that Sacrifice, well and good, we partake in the fruits of the all-prevailing intercession ; if we
stay away, then we show Him that we think we can do without the Atonement.

It is not a different sacrifice which is offered here in
England from what is offered in France, and Spain, and
Russia, and Greece, and America, and Asia, but it is one and
the same.   Just as every pond and drop of still water on a
summer's day reflects the golden sun, and it is not one sun in
this pond, and another sun in that pool, and another sun in

that still brook, and another that sparkles out of that rain-drop, but it is the same sun that shines reflected in each; and as it is not a part of the sun here, and a part of the sun there, but the whole sun in each, so does every altar in Christendom reflect the Sacrifice of CHRIST, whole and entire, and every priest offers to GOD the FATHER the same All-holy, Divine Victim.

And just as when one man is speaking to a crowd, his words fall on each ear, whole and unbroken, so that one does not hear one word, another hear another word, the third again hear another word, but his one sentence is heard by every one, whole and entire :—so it is with the Eucharist, to each, the virtue of CHRIST'S presence descends, and each communicant receives CHRIST entire.

In every sacrifice there are these four things to be considered. 1. To whom the sacrifice is offered. 2. By whom it is offered. 3. What it is that is offered. And 4. For whom it is offered.

1. Now in the Sacrifice of CHRIST'S death on Calvary,—and it is the same with the Sacrifice of the Altar,—the One to whom it is offered is GOD the FATHER, and it is offered to Him to turn away His anger from us, when He is justly wroth with us for our sins.

2. It is offered by CHRIST Himself, "He is a Priest for ever," we are told. And when S. John saw Him in heaven, He was standing in priestly robe, ever making intercession for us.

He freely offered of His own will.

"Sacrifice and offering Thou wouldest not,"—that is, such as were under the law. "Then said I, Lo, I come to fulfil Thy will, O GOD,"—more properly rendered, to make the *freewill* offering, because the sacrifices and offerings which were of *obligation* displeased GOD, being offered with hard and unloving hearts. And then follow the memorable words of the apostle, " He taketh away the first, that He may establish the second." He takes away the empty sacrifices of *obligation* of the old law, that He may establish, or make to last for ever, the *freewill* offering and sacrifice of JESUS CHRIST. " By the which will"—properly freewill offering— " we are sanctified through the offering of the Body of JESUS CHRIST once for all." (Heb. x. 10, 11.)

3. Next, what is offered. The body and soul of CHRIST. "Sacrifice and offering Thou wouldest not,"—which are offered by the law,—"but a Body hast Thou prepared Me," CHRIST says. And when this is repeated, the words are changed, but not the sense, "Sacrifice and offering Thou wouldest not, then said I, Lo, I come to make a freewill offering." That offering is the Body which GOD the FATHER had prepared in the womb of blessed Mary.

And not only is the Body of CHRIST offered, but also His soul. "When He shall make His soul an offering for sin," is the expression of the prophet. (Isaiah liii. 10.)

4. Lastly, the sacrifice was offered for us, for our redemption, for the remission of our sins, for our restoration.

" O GOD, Who in this wondrous Sacrament hast left unto us a memorial of Thy Passion, grant us so to venerate the sacred mysteries of Thy Body and Blood, that we may always perceive in ourselves the fruits of our redemption."

XV.

THE RESURRECTION.

" Since by man came death : by man came also the resurrection of the dead. For as in Adam all die: even so in Christ shall all be made alive."—1 Cor. xv. 21, 22.

OUR LORD JESUS CHRIST rose from the grave on Easter Day. After His death on Good Friday, He was taken down from the cross and laid in a grave. On Easter Day in the morning He broke away from that grave.

It was the same LORD who had been laid there who rose. The Jews had set soldiers to watch the grave ; and had set their seals on the stone. The soldiers and the sealed stone could not restrain the rising CHRIST.

It was the same body that had been laid in the grave that rose from it. When the angel rolled back the stone, and the spring sun shone into the tomb, the body of CHRIST was gone. The napkin and linen shroud were there, but not CHRIST's body. Therefore His soul did not leave the dead body that it might assume another body.

Again, when He appeared after His resurrection to the Apostles, He showed them His hands and feet, wherein were the marks of the nails, that they might see for themselves that it was the crucified JESUS who had hung on the Cross.

Nor was this rising a mere waking after a long trance. He had really died. The soldier's spear had pierced His side, and the lance-head had cut into His heart. Now He is risen He calls to doubting Thomas, " Reach hither thy finger, and behold My hands ; and reach hither thy hand, and thrust it into My side ; and be not faithless, but believing."

So far then is clear. The man's body and man's soul of JESUS which He had taken of Mary, which had lived on earth and had died on Calvary, rose on Easter Day. The man's soul, which had, by death, been separated from the body, came back to it. And now body, soul, and divinity are united never again to be divided. As CHRIST rose, so did He afterwards ascend into heaven, as He ascended into heaven, so does He now reign at the right hand of the FATHER. As He now reigns, so will He come on the clouds to judge the world ; as He comes to judge, so will He be for endless ages, everlastingly GOD and man.

Now why did CHRIST rise from the dead ?

He rose to complete our salvation ; for, when we see CHRIST the Second Adam, the new head of the human race, overcome death, we may be sure that the victory over death which is the consequence of sin, was part of His design, as well as the conquest over sin itself.

We know that Adam, by his transgression, brought death into the world ; and death passed upon all men, for all are descended from Adam. If Adam had begotten children before the fall, these children and their descendants would have inherited his innocent nature, and therewith freedom from pain and death. But because he begat children after his fall, therefore all his race partook of his fallen nature, subject to death. Now how is it that we derive our liability to death from Adam ? It is through partaking of his sinful flesh. We all of us derive by birth our flesh from Adam. You derive your body and blood from the womb of your mother, your mother derived hers from her mother, and so

back, and back to Eve into whose nature the poison of sin
was introduced by her fall.

During the plague of London many instances occurred of
mothers being attacked with the pestilence as they were
approaching their confinement, and it was found that the
babes they bore all came into the world with the plague
poison in their veins, so that after a few days the poor little
things died of the disorder also. So the plague poison of
death was taken into the veins of Eve by her transgression,
and her children inherited it from her, and so it has been
transmitted on from generation to generation. You have
the poison in your veins, I have it in mine. When sickness
comes on you, then it is beginning its work, when death
supervenes, then it has accomplished its work.

If we were to discover an island in which were people
who never died, we might be quite sure that they did not
derive their nature from Adam and Eve.

Now, I beg you clearly to bear in mind why it is that we
are subject to death ; or you will not understand how it is
that we are made able to overcome death.

We derive our liability to death from the fact that we
have inherited our bodies from Adam and Eve, our flesh
and blood we derive from the death-poisoned flesh and
blood of Adam and Eve.

But we know that our LORD JESUS CHRIST is called the
Second Adam. " For since by man came death, by man
came also the Resurrection of the dead." That is to say,
we know that through JESUS CHRIST the head of the human
race for *good*, as Adam was the head of the human race for
evil, we shall obtain power to rise from the grave, and overcome death. Adam brought death upon the whole human
race. CHRIST is come to offer victory over death to the

whole human race. CHRIST is not come to force it on us, for you will remember that we are endowed with free-will, and He does nothing without the co-operation of our wills.

We believe then that, through the victory of CHRIST over death, we shall be enabled to wake up after a brief separation of body and soul to an endless life of joy; that though for a while the body must die, yet that the body cannot wholly die. In it is a power of revival, a germ of renewal; it will not be like a dead grain, but like one in which is a spring of life to make it in due time to start up in fresh vigour and bloom and beauty.

And we know that as " CHRIST being risen from the dead dieth no more, death hath no more dominion over Him," so those who, through Him, overcome death, and rise, will rise to an eternal life, they also will die no more ; death will have no more dominion over them.

But now comes the question, how are we to partake of the nature of CHRIST so as to obtain that new principle of life ?

It is very evident that as we derive death from Adam by partaking of his fallen nature, so we must derive the power of resurrection and victory over death by partaking of CHRIST'S risen nature.

It is very evident that as we derive our liability to die from the death-poisoned flesh and blood of Adam, so we must obtain our power to rise from the death-conquering flesh and blood of CHRIST. Adam's body was poisoned, and has transmitted the poison to us ; CHRIST'S body is the antidote, or medicine driving out the poison, must be given to us, so as to expel what Adam introduced.

It was for this purpose that CHRIST instituted His Sacrament of the Holy Communion, in which our death-poisoned bodies should be able to touch and receive into them His death-conquering Body, which might drive the poison out of our veins, and impregnate our systems with the power to overcome death.

Observe, our bodies are death-stricken through an actual participation in the death-stricken body of Adam, so our bodies must be healed by an actual participation in the life-giving Body of CHRIST.

Now if the Holy Communion were a mere memorial of CHRIST's death, it might do good to our souls, but it would do no good to our bodies, it would leave our bodies just as poisoned as before.

In fact, the Holy Communion as a sacrifice or memorial of CHRIST's death, does very great good to our souls ; and again, as a sacrament, it is grace-giving to our souls ; and so are other sacraments grace-giving, and other things do good to our souls. But the fall of Adam not only hurt our souls, but it hurt our bodies also, so that we want not only the medicine of Divine grace to heal our sinful souls, but we want also the medicine of a regenerating body to heal our death-stricken flesh.

Nor would the Holy Communion be of any avail for this purpose if the elements remained mere bread and wine, for what possible good would bread and wine do in the sacrament more than on any other occasion? No. In order that they may become a medicine to our bodies, they must be changed verily and indeed into the risen Body and Blood of JESUS CHRIST: into that very Body that rose from the grave on Easter Day, because it is that Body only which has conquered death, and it is that Body only which can infuse into our bodies the power to rise in like manner.

Now you will see at once the meaning of our LORD's

address in the sixth chapter of S. John's Gospel: "The bread of GOD is He which cometh down from heaven, and giveth life unto the world. I am the Bread of Life. Your fathers did eat manna in the wilderness, and are dead. This is the bread which cometh down from heaven, that a man may eat thereof, and not die. I am the living bread which came down from heaven; if any man eat of this bread he shall live for ever: and the bread that I will give is My flesh, which I will give for the life of the world. The Jews therefore strove among themselves, saying, How can this man give us his flesh to eat? Then JESUS said unto them, Verily, verily, I say unto you, Except ye eat the flesh of the Son of Man, and drink His blood, ye have no life in you. Whoso eateth My flesh, and drinketh My blood, hath eternal life; and I will raise him up at the last day. For My flesh is meat indeed, and My blood is drink indeed."

How very simple and intelligible all this is, if we only understand the close connexion that exists between the resurrection of CHRIST and the Holy Communion! But if we are ignorant of this, or disbelieve it, all is a jumble, there is nothing in our LORD's great address on this occasion, but something to be explained away.

GOD open your understandings, my dear brethren, that you may perceive how important is this mystery; and that you may profit by the means provided for you of receiving into your bodies the leaven of eternal life.

XVI.

THE GREAT FORTY DAYS.

" He showed Himself alive after His passion by many infallible proofs, being seen of them forty days, and speaking of the things pertaining to the kingdom of God."—Acts i. 3.

JESUS CHRIST spent forty days on earth after He rose from the grave, before He went up into heaven and a cloud received Him out of the sight of the Apostles.

What was He doing during those forty days? Very important days they must have been. He had died on the Cross, had been buried, and was risen, and the faith of His Apostles was confirmed in Him in a way in which it never had been confirmed before by His miracles. They were prepared for something more ; for some fuller teaching, some clearer instructions in the purposes of GOD, some further insight into the great plan of Redemption. Before CHRIST died, it was not possible for them to understand the mystery of the Atonement, but now that He had died and was risen, their minds were open to receive instruction as to *Why* CHRIST had died.

Before CHRIST rose from the grave, it was not possible for them to understand what CHRIST would do, and what was His purpose, in descending into the grave and rising from it after three days. But after He had risen, then they would naturally want to know *Why* He had risen, and so would be naturally ready to receive instruction in that mystery, which could not have been made clear to their understandings before.

Now we are told in Holy Scripture that JESUS CHRIST employed those forty days in teaching the Apostles "the things concerning the kingdom of heaven." The kingdom of heaven means that kingdom whose King would be in heaven, from whence also it would look for His return to drive out of it all that offends, and to make it altogether heavenly. That kingdom is the Church.

CHRIST taught the Apostles all that concerned His Church. Before His resurrection, when He went about among men generally, His teaching was general, it was for all men to listen to. But now, after His resurrection, He does not go about among men generally, but gathers round Him His Apostles with the brethren only. His teaching is no longer general, but special;—that is, it applies to His Church only. Before, He had dwelt in His teaching on the great truths of GOD's nature, His own mission, and the moral law. He had laid the foundations : He had called men to the truth. Now He spake to those who had heard His call, who had gathered into His Church. His teaching was now to those who were to be the rulers in that kingdom which He had come on earth to found, and which they were to devote their lives in extending throughout the world.

Now what are the things the Apostles would want to know. They would need to receive instructions as to how the Church was to be constituted, that is, how it was to be governed, what were to be the orders of ministers or officers in that kingdom, what and how discipline was to be enforced in it ; what was the faith that they were to teach to the world, that Andrew might not teach in Russia different truths from Thomas in India, Peter at Rome, Mark in Egypt ; but that all, everywhere, might teach the same faith, neither more nor less, so that converts in Russia and India and Rome and Egypt might all believe the same truths and transmit the same to future generations.

Then again they would need instruction in how the Sacraments were to be administered ; those links which were to unite man with GOD, so that all members of the Church everywhere might receive grace through the same channels, and lest through the error or fault of some Apostles their converts should have fewer means of grace than the converts of other Apostles.

All this, then, CHRIST taught His Apostles in the forty days between His Resurrection and Ascension. And all this teaching was to be the heritage of His Church for ever. Our Faith, our Sacramental system, our Apostolic ministry, —are all the fruit of that teaching.

This teaching was not written down in the New Testament. There was no need to write it down. The teaching in the Gospels is that which is general, to call all to the acknowledgment of JESUS CHRIST. When they have acknowledged Him, they will enter His kingdom, and as members of His Church they receive the special teaching CHRIST gave in these forty days.

Look at S. Paul's cathedral, and you know what was in the mind of the architect who planned it, you do not want a minute description of it from his pen, when you have the thing itself. Look at the Catholic Church, and you know what was in the mind of CHRIST when He planned it. We have not an account of all He taught His masons who were to build up His Church ; we do not want that teaching, for we have the result, the Church itself. The Church itself is the living Gospel of the " Great Forty Days." We know perfectly well what CHRIST taught then, better than if it had been committed to paper, when we see what is the constitution of the Church, what its Faith, what its Orders, what its Sacraments.

It is a mistake to suppose that the Bible contains everything a Christian is to believe set out in so many plain words. It gives us the broad outlines of the truth, all that is necessary to call us into the Church, and then it leaves us to the teaching of the Church. You say to your child, "Go to school." And by sending the child to school you do all that is necessary for its instruction. So the Bible says, "Hear the Church," and sends us into the Church to learn the truth, and thus the Bible does all for us that is necessary for our instruction in the Faith.

S. John tells us, "There are also many other things which JESUS did, the which, if they should be written every one, I suppose that even the world itself could not contain the books that should be written." What CHRIST taught in the forty days was among those things unrecorded by pen, but perpetuated in the living practice of the Church.

Now after JESUS CHRIST had taught the Truth to His Church, and all the Apostles understood clearly what they were to believe and teach ; then CHRIST breathed on them and said, "Receive ye the HOLY GHOST." He had told them how the Sacraments were to be administered, now He gives them power to administer them. Next He said, "Go ye into all the world, and preach the Gospel to every creature." Here He gave to His Apostles *mission*, or authority, that they might go, not in their own name, and with their own authority, but in His Name, and with His authority ; that they might go as ambassadors, formally commissioned by Him to the whole world.

Do you know what an ambassador means ? When the Queen wants to send a message to the French government, or the Emperor of Germany, or the Emperor of Austria, or the King of Belgium, she sends a man with the message, she commissions him, and he goes with his commission under the royal seal to the prince or government to which he is sent. If a man comes—say to the Emperor of Germany, and says, " I am sent by Queen Victoria with a message to you," he is at once asked for his commission. How can he prove that he has been sent? If he produces his commission, well and good, he is listened to. If he has not got his commission, he is sent to the right-about. Now by the words " Go ye into all the world, and preach the Gospel to every creature," CHRIST gave their mission to the Apostles, that they might go as His ambassadors to the whole world.

But He knew very well that the eleven could not themselves teach the whole world, it was not possible for them to traverse Europe, Asia, Africa, and America, and teach every living man, woman and child. It was necessary that they should have assistants as they needed them, and successors to fill their places when they died. If an ambassador from the Queen is on his way to Berlin, and feels that he is too ill to proceed, and is at the point of death, he finds some trusty person, and he puts the commission and the message into his hands, and sends him on at once to bear the message to the Emperor of Germany. So, if the Apostles were unable to fulfil the task themselves, they were to put their commission and the message into the hands of other trusty men, and send them on.

This is precisely what they did. They ordained others, and so bishops and priests were spread throughout the world, with their commissions in their hands to show that they have been sent. Look here. This is what is called my "Letters of Orders." It is my commission, received from the bishop, to tell all that I do not come in my own name, that I am not here on my own authority, but that I have been sent here by the bishop. And the bishop was sent by other bishops, who were sent in regular succession from the Apostles, who received their commission direct from JESUS CHRIST.

Now some might say: "How can we be sure that the mission given by JESUS CHRIST has not died out?" To make quite sure that such would not be the case, JESUS CHRIST added this promise: "Lo, I am with you always even unto the end of the world." In those words He assured us that He would be with His ministry, continuing to it the same authority, the same power, that He gave originally to the Apostles. "Lo, I am with you, Apostles, and with all whom you shall send, and those who in turn shall fill their place, even unto the end of the world." And before that, He had promised most solemnly, "This generation shall not pass away till all be fulfilled; heaven and earth shall pass away, but My words shall not pass away." That is to say, though everything changes, the world waxes old, and all political institutions and social customs alter, yet be not afraid, one thing I promise shall never disappear, My sacred ministry, commissioned by Me to preach the Gospel to every creature, empowered by Me to perform valid sacraments, that ministry continued in a spiritual generation from age to age shall not pass away till all be fulfilled.

I think it will be well to tell you plainly why I am here speaking to you from this pulpit, looking after your souls in this parish. This you know is a Crown living, and I was nominated to it by the Queen. But the Queen did not give me authority over your souls and commit to me the charge of feeding you with the Bread of Life and the Word of GOD. She could not do this, for she has not received authority from GOD for this. The Queen exercises authority over men's bodies and possessions, but not over their immortal souls. What I receive from the Crown is a right to receive the tithes from the farmers in this parish, a right, that is, to draw so much money from the place. If tithe were taken away, as it has been in some places, as in West Mersea, and appropriated to some layman, then, in that case, you see the Crown allows that layman to draw so much money from the place, instead of the incumbent. I believe the great tithe of West Mersea has just been bought by a barrister in London, but lately it was enjoyed by an oyster-merchant.

This then is what I derive from the Crown, a right to the tithe of this parish. But I derive my authority as shepherd of your souls, not from the Crown, but from JESUS CHRIST, through His officer, the bishop. The Queen, I said, exercises authority over men's bodies and possessions. Her kingdom is thus constituted; it is earthly and temporal. But JESUS CHRIST exercises authority over men's souls. His kingdom is heavenly and spiritual. So JESUS CHRIST sent me to you. I am His ambassador to East Mersea. When I was ordained by a bishop, I was given the HOLY GHOST to empower me to celebrate the Sacraments; and that bishop sent me to minister to the souls in a parish in Yorkshire. But now I am here in Essex. When I was instituted to this living, I went to the Bishop of Rochester and knelt before him, and he laid his hands on my head, and gave me authority to shepherd the souls in this place. He exercised spiritual authority, because he is an officer in CHRIST's kingdom, and he executes his office not on his own authority, but on that of CHRIST, from Whom he derives it by that spiritual generation which CHRIST promised should never die out.

I dare say some think, "Well but if the grace and authority of CHRIST have been thus handed on from age to age, it must have altered or been lost on the way."

No. We have CHRIST's promise that it shall not. Take a Bible. Give it to the first child at the head of a class in school. Bid him pass it to the next, and so on and on and on till it comes to the last boy, who surrenders the book back into your hand. Well. Is there one word less, one letter less, in that Bible now that it has passed through the hands of fifty boys, than when you gave it to the first? No, it is the same, there is not one word or letter more, there is not one word or letter less.

So is it with the Grace of GOD handed on from age to age in the ministry of His Church, it is the same grace now that was given at first to the Apostles, it will be the same when restored to CHRIST by those He finds, at His Second Coming, ministering to His chosen people.

> "CHRIST is gone up, yet ere He passed
> From earth in heaven to reign,
> He formed one Holy Church to last
> Till He should come again.
>
> "His Twelve Apostles first He made
> His ministers of Grace,
> And they their hands on others laid
> To fill in turn their place.
>
> "So age by age, and year by year
> His grace was handed on,
> And still the Holy Church is here
> Although her LORD is gone."

XVII.

THE ASCENSION.

" And it came to pass, while He blessed them, He was parted from them, and carried up into heaven."—S. Luke xxiv. 51.

I HAD so much to say to you last Sunday about what JESUS CHRIST did on earth during the forty days between His resurrection and His ascension, that I left myself no time to speak to you about the great truths involved in the ascension of JESUS CHRIST.

I shall speak of these now.

When CHRIST had finished these forty days, He led His disciples on the way to Bethany as far as the Mount of Olives, and there He lifted up His hands to bless them, and as He blessed them He rose in the air, up, up, into the blue sky, and a white cloud hid Him from their sight. He had gone up into heaven. He would not come again to earth in His human form till the second coming at the Last Day.

Now there are several things for you to observe about the ascension of JESUS CHRIST.

He went up into heaven in the same body in which He rose from the grave, the same human body in which He had died. It was the same body that had been born of Mary at Bethlehem which now ascended gloriously to the highest heavens, and in that same body did JESUS CHRIST sit down at the right hand of GOD the FATHER.

CHRIST in His Man's body, with His human soul, went up into heaven, and in heaven is CHRIST still in His man's body, with His human soul, from which He will never be parted eternally.   When He took flesh in Mary's womb, He united *for ever* the Manhood and the Godhead.

When He comes again in the clouds of heaven, He will come in His human body.   When we see Him in His eternal and glorious kingdom, we shall see the Man who died and rose again, and ascended into heaven.'   Never, never through long ages, will that body be cast away.   "Those dear tokens of His Passion still His glorious body wears," to rejoice the saints, and fill their hearts to overflow through an eternity.

JESUS CHRIST went up into heaven :

1. To prepare a place for us.   "I go to prepare a place for you."   You know the feeling one has in preparing for the coming of a friend or a relation.   I was in one of your cottages the other day.   The son was expected back from a long voyage.   He had been to sea five years.   For five years his mother and father had not seen him.   The mother was busy getting the room tidy for him, the father was gone to get a bit of meat for the dinner on his return.   What delight there was to both in making ready for the sailor's return. The room was dusted, the chairs and wardrobe polished up, the bit of carpet had been newly patched, there was a tumbler of roses on the table, and a pot of mignionette in the window.   The father had dug up the plant of mignionette and potted it on purpose to make the room pleasant for his dear boy.   GOD bless them all !   Happy hearts rejoicing together !   But oh ! what a pleasure that long preparation for the expected one.

Do you think it is not a pleasure to JESUS CHRIST to make ready His mansions in heaven for us, who are bone of His bone, and flesh of His flesh ? I know it is. His is a human heart. Whatsoever sweet, good, happy feelings throb in our hearts throb also in His. How dear we are to Him we scarcely can understand unless we meditate on all He has done for us. And now in heaven what is He doing? He is devising some new delight for us ; creating some new beauty. Look up at Him on the throne of heaven, His bright, sweet face musing, "What more can I do? What will best please so and so?" And then He calls into being some new loveliness, opens some new fount of pleasure.

When you go into market on Saturday, you look about and buy something for the children at home. You are thinking what will best please little Mary, or little John, and are quite delighted when you hit on something you know will make them dance and clap their hands with pleasure, when you return with the things.

Jesus Christ is human, His heart is human. That dear human heart beating up there above that blue sky, and all those white fleecy clouds, feels the same pleasure in providing for us His children such good things as will most gratify us. He has gone to prepare home for us, to make home happy, beautiful, glorious. Oh ! for the day when the door is thrown open, and we rush in and see what He has prepared for us !

2. Jesus Christ went up into heaven to send the Holy Ghost down upon us. That gift which He gave to the Apostles for a special purpose on the day of the Ascension, when He breathed on them, He was about to communicate to them in a more abundant and more general way on the Day of Pentecost, and not on them only, His first bishops, but on all His Church. There were two outpourings of the Holy Ghost; the first at the Ascension, on the Apostles

to consecrate them for the ministry; the second at Whitsuntide, on all, not for any special purpose, but generally.

And that Holy SPIRIT which was then given is given still, as it filled the house where all were sitting, so now it fills the whole Church of GOD.

3. JESUS CHRIST went up into heaven to assume the dominion, the crown and the throne of His kingdom,—that kingdom He had just founded, and into which He had breathed life.

And now what do we mean when we say that JESUS CHRIST, our risen and ascended LORD, is king and head of His Church?

We mean that from Him alone streams every grace, all power to do good, to think what is right, to act consistently with our profession. But we mean more than this. We mean that access to the FATHER is through Him alone. We mean that, whereas before CHRIST'S ascension, before He took the reins of government into His hands, GOD could be reached, and grace could be given, in a purely spiritual way, *now*, on the contrary, CHRIST being head over all to the Church, GOD can only be reached through the GOD-Man, and grace can only be given through the GOD-Man. We are living under quite another dispensation. The Jewish was spiritual only. The law of this dispensation is the spiritual through the material. That is, the spiritual and the material are indissolubly united, the inward and spiritual cannot be separated from the outward and visible. Outside the Church, the kingdom of CHRIST, GOD may deal with men in the same way as before, in a purely spiritual way. But all within the Church have passed under the rule of CHRIST the king, and His rule is, that all grace flows through outward and visible means.

All CHRIST'S dealings with man accord with His nature. He is GOD and Man. As GOD, invisible, spiritual; as Man, visible, material; that you can touch, and see, and hear. So in all His dealings with us, there is the form you can touch, or see, or hear, and there is the invisible, spiritual part, which is Divine, which you cannot perceive with your senses.

4. JESUS CHRIST is gone up into heaven to intercede for us with the FATHER. As men sin, so does He plead, showing the FATHER His wounds, and obtaining for us those good things which of ourselves we are not worthy to ask. He is our advocate there. What a source of hope, of confidence. We have one to plead our cause who has suffered like us, has been tempted like us, who knows the weakness of mortal nature, the violence of passion.

5. JESUS CHRIST is gone up on high to give us hope. " I will surely assemble, O Jacob, all of thee; I will surely gather the remnant of Israel: I will put them together as the sheep of Bozrah, as the flock in the midst of their fold: they shall make great noise by reason of the multitude of men. The breaker is come up before them: they have broken up, and have passed through the gate, and are gone out by it; and their king shall pass before them, and the LORD on the head of them." (Micah ii. 12, 13.)

Such were the words of the prophet Micah long before. He foretold that CHRIST would be the head of His people, He their King would go before them, He the breaker of the gates of brass, Who has smitten the bars of iron in sunder would go through the gate of Paradise and the multitude of men the remnant of Israel, the assembled of Jacob, would be gathered and go in with the LORD at their head.

Before CHRIST died Paradise was closed, but now the

fiery sword of the cherub turning every way no longer keeps the gate, CHRIST enters in, and His people flow in after Him. He has the key of David to unlock heaven, He, a second Joshua, leads the way into the promised land. Thus we are made possessors of Paradise by the ascension of JESUS CHRIST. "Where He who is my portion reigns, there I believe that I shall reign," says S. Augustine ; "Where CHRIST who is my flesh is glorified, there shall I be glorious, where CHRIST who is of my blood triumphs, there I feel that I shall triumph. And though I am a sinner, yet will I trust in His abundant grace, and all prevailing intercession."

Now from these great truths contained in the doctrine of the Ascension of JESUS CHRIST, there flow certain consequences, or applications to us.

1. CHRIST has gone up on high to prepare a place for us. Therefore here we have no continuing city, but we look for one that is eternal, in the heavens, whose maker and builder is GOD. Our home is where CHRIST is, and there let our affections be. Here let us live as exiles and wanderers looking forward to, and preparing for that blessed time when we shall be called home.

Our life must be heavenly, as our home is heavenly. Our thoughts must be turned on how we can live here as members of that heavenly kingdom, keeping its laws, obeying its king, that He may recognize us as His own true subjects.

2. CHRIST is gone up on high to receive gifts for men, to dispense to men the HOLY GHOST. Therefore to Him must we turn in time of need, He alone is our refuge and strength, able to succour to the uttermost all those that come . to Him.

3. CHRIST is gone up on high to reign as head over His

Church, that is, to communicate grace according to His nature, through outward channels, veiled in visible forms. Therefore we learn to value Sacraments, because they are the means whereby we touch CHRIST, and partake of grace. In them the outward part corresponds with the visible manhood of CHRIST, 'and the inward part corresponds with the invisible Godhead of CHRIST.

4. CHRIST is gone up on high to intercede for us. Therefore we can come boldly to the throne of grace, knowing that we have not a high priest who cannot be touched with the feeling of our infirmities, but was in all points tempted as we are, suffered as we suffer, knows our weakness, and, being of our nature, loves us and compassionates us, as brothers, and is ready to make reconciliation for all such as turn to the FATHER in true repentance, and seek remission of guilt through His blood.

5. And lastly: CHRIST went up on high to lead the way for us, to open Paradise to all believers. Surely, therefore, with that hope set before us, we can run with patience the race set before us, looking unto JESUS, the author and finisher of our faith.

XVIII.

THE MAKING UP OF THE NUMBER OF THE ELECT.

" When the Son of Man shall come in His glory, and all the holy Angels with Him, then shall He sit upon the throne of His glory: and before Him shall be gathered all nations: and He shall separate them one from another, as a shepherd divideth his sheep from the goats."—S. Matth. xxv. 31, 32.

WE know a great deal about the Second Coming of JESUS CHRIST.

We know that His first coming was in humility, the second will be with power and great glory. We know that His first coming was to save, His second will be to judge.

We know also what will be the signs of this second coming; how that Antichrist will appear, and that faith will have died out, everywhere save in the Church, and therein even many will be lukewarm; how also that there will be remarkable wars, earthquakes, and signs in heaven.

We know also many of the circumstances attending the second coming, that the Cross, the sign of the Son of Man, going before Him, as a standard before a king, will blaze in heaven; that then a trumpet will sound, and all men will rise to give account of their works; that CHRIST will appear in heaven, sitting on a white cloud, in the midst of His Angels and the Apostles, and that then He will judge all men.

But there is one very important thing we do not know, and that is, *when* the second coming will take place, whether at cock-crow, or at morning dawn, or at noon, or at eve, or at midnight. Nor do we know what time of the year it will take place, at Advent or Christmas, or Easter. Nor do we know the year of CHRIST'S coming. "Of that day and that hour knoweth no man," said our LORD.

But there is one thing about the time we do know; and that is,—the second coming will take place as soon as the number of the elect is made up.

Understand me. GOD has fixed on a certain number which will be admitted to everlasting joy. That number is unalterable, He will not change it, and cut it smaller, or make it a higher figure to let in more. The number has been fixed from all eternity. As soon as the number is made up, *then* the end will come. Not a moment before, not a moment after. Every year, nay, every day, the number that remains to be made up gets smaller, for some have finished their course, have fought the good fight.

This number that remains to be made up gets less and less. One day it is twenty, then it is ten, then five, then two, then only one; and the moment that one has reached the measure of perfection, the end will come.

The measure of perfection. Not only is there a certain predeterminate number of the elect, but there is also a measure of perfection for each Christian, some have a very high standard, some a very low one, but to each the measure of perfection is the highest possible goodness attainable by that person with the faculties and opportunities he has. All have not the same faculties, all have not the same opportunities; to whom much is given of him much will be required.

But to return to the number of the elect. Some day, the coming of the end of all things will depend on one person.

Till that one person is perfected, CHRIST cannot come, the
world must roll on its course. Possibly that person may
be one utterly unknown to, or disregarded by the world.
It may be some poor old woman dying in a garret in a
wretched cottage. The wind is blowing in at the broken
window, ill stopped with an old stocking. She lies on the
floor with only a dirty rag to cover her; she has no nourish-
ing food, no medicine, she dies in solitude, amidst dire
poverty. Yet the world waits on that old woman, JESUS
CHRIST waits on that old woman. Till she has conquered
in the last struggle of her rebellious will, and has perfectly
surrendered herself to the will of GOD, till she has reached
her measure of perfection, the number cannot be made up,
the sky cannot burst asunder and display the white throne
of the great Judge.

Or, the coming may depend on some sailor boy. His
ship is in port, he is allowed on shore, with money in his
pocket. In the lowest and wickedest part of a great sea-
port town, he is surrounded with temptations to evil. Will
he yield? will he resist? Oh, Jack! the world, the living,
the dead, the Angels, the Apostles, JESUS CHRIST wait on
the result.

You know, some of you who have been to sea, what are
the perils surrounding the lad at that moment. But he
knows not, the world knows not, ay! the Angels and
Apostles know not, that the coming of the Son of Man
this day depends upon Jack's conduct at this moment.

Here in the West of London is a grand Court ball.
What a blaze of light! The powdered coachmen on their
hammercloths drive up to the great doors, down jump the
lackeys, help ladies in silks and plumes and diamonds to
alight. *Here*, the ball-room festooned, odorous, dazzling

with colour, light and beauty. *There*, at the London Docks, a sailor lad in a dark lane assailed by temptation.

What know they at the Court ball that it depends on that sailor boy whether they are to dance their dance out to-night?

Lady Blanche, that fair young girl there, gliding along in the dance with bright face and joyous heart—does she know that may-be next moment the end will have come?

Turn your eyes from the light, and look at the dark lane once more. Temptation is terrible, but the lad has not received the grace of GOD in vain. He uses it. He conquers.

Hush! All is over. The earth reels as a drunkard, the trumpet is calling through the night sky. The dead are rising out of all the churchyards, the dancers in their satins and feathers stand blank, looking up, and the glare of the cross in the black night sky is on their uplifted faces. Shoulder to shoulder they stand. Lady Blanche has a ragged urchin on one side of her, who peeped through the railings at her half-an-hour ago as she alighted from her carriage, and on the other side a risen man in a winding-sheet flapping in the wind.

But had the sailor lad yielded to the temptation, his chance would have passed to some one else, and the Judgment be delayed a little longer.

Now, my brethren, is not this a striking thought? We know not how near the Number is to completion, we know not how soon our chance may be snatched from us.

Do not forget, to all of us a chance is afforded of being of that number. As soon as we were baptized we were offered that. The opportunity is ours if we choose to seize it.

I

To you, to me, to every baptized Christian GOD gives a
chance of being of the number of His Elect; a chance
denied to others. If we use our opportunity, accept the
offer; then well for us :—our names are written in heaven.
If we let our chance go by, neglect our opportunity, put on
one side the offer made us, then GOD turns to some one
else.

How do you know, but that your chance, which you hold
so light and allow to slip from you, will be transferred to
some Red Indian, now skulking among the pines of Canada,
pursuing the elk, and thinking nothing of CHRIST and salvation. One day a missionary will teach him and baptize him,
and then the opportunity is offered to him. What opportunity? Why that which had been John Brown's of Mersea,
Essex; but which John Brown flung away from him as
worthless.

At the Day of the Last Judgment he who has lost his
chance will see the one to whom that chance was next
offered, and who accepted it, enter into life, whilst he himself
remains shut out in darkness.

I need hardly tell you on what conditions the chance is
given you. The conditions are very plainly set forth in
your Catechism, and in the Baptismal Service. You have
certain things to believe and certain things to do. Believe
with all your heart, do GOD's will with all your might,
assisted by Sacramental Grace, and your name is written in
heaven. GOD will keep His promise. He will not with-
draw from you what He has covenanted to give you.

And now in conclusion. "Watch, for ye know neither
the day nor the hour wherein the Son of Man cometh."
Watch your own selves, watch that your faith is right, watch
that you are keeping the commandments of GOD both in

the letter and in the spirit.   Watch your acts, watch your
words, watch your thoughts.   Watch that your repentance for
past transgressions be sincere, watch unto prayer, learn to
have a watchful heart against all the snares of the devil,
so that, watching, you may be found ready when the LORD
comes, and being found ready, He may admit you into His
rest.

XIX.

THE MISSION OF THE HOLY GHOST.

*" God hath from the beginning chosen you to salvation, through the
sanctification of the Spirit and belief of the truth."*—2 Thess. ii. 13.

WHEN GOD made Adam of the dust of the earth, Adam lay
on the ground without life and motion.   There were the
eyes, but they saw not, the ears, but they heard not, the
feet, but they walked not, the hands, but they handled not.

Then GOD breathed into him the Breath of Life, and all
at once—man lived and moved.   The eyes looked about
and saw things plainly.   The ears heard the sounds of the
birds, and the wind rustling the leaves, Adam started to his
feet and walked, put forth his hands, and grasped the fruits
and the flowers of Eden.

Years passed away.   One day Adam lay down on the
earth, his eyes closed, his hands and feet became motionless,
he ceased to hear.   The beautiful machinery of his body
had ceased to act.   The breath of life had been withdrawn.
He was dead.

What was it made Adam live and move and think and
see and hear and act?

It was the Breath of GOD in him. And that breath was his Life. Without it, he was a mere piece of beautiful clock-work put skilfully together. The breath of life was that which set him in motion and kept him in activity, and made all his members perform their allotted parts.

Now before our LORD JESUS CHRIST went up into heaven, in the great forty days between His Resurrection and His Ascension, He formed His Church. That is, He was with His Apostles, and He taught them what they were to believe and teach to all the world, what were to be the means of communicating with Him, that is, how they were to obtain power, and authority, and grace from Him. We call these means by one word,—Sacraments. Well ; He taught them what the Sacraments were for, and how they were to be performed.

And then He breathed on them, and said, "Receive ye the HOLY GHOST."

He had made His Church, planned and arranged it all in beautiful order, but it was lifeless, like Adam. All the parts of it were fitted together, all the sacramental veins and the doctrinal joints were fashioned, but there was no life. Then He breathed—and all at once, His Church started into life.

Before that, the Apostles might have baptized, and it would have been a mere sign, no grace would have flowed ; *after* that, they baptized, and the HOLY GHOST came to regenerate.

Before that, the Apostles might have gone forth preaching, but their word would have fallen dead and flat ; *after* that, the HOLY GHOST gave them utterance, and multitudes heard and believed.

Before that, they might have taken bread and wine in remembrance of the death of CHRIST, and blessed and broken, and it would have remained mere bread and mere wine. It would have been only an edifying ceremony, a pious memorial of CHRIST. *After* that, they took bread and wine and brake, and the HOLY GHOST descended, so that these became, verily and indeed, the Body and Blood of CHRIST.

Before that, they might have said to the sinner, "Go, thy sins are forgiven thee," and the sinner would have gone away yet in his sins. *After* that, they spoke the absolving word, and by the power of the HOLY GHOST the Blood of CHRIST was applied to guilty souls cleansing them from all sin.

Before that, they might have united the hands of two people who desired to be man and wife, but it would have been a mere registrar's-office sort of marriage, a proclaiming of the fact to the public that these two were man and wife. *After* that, it was very different, something was given,—the HOLY GHOST was present to confer grace on the couple to live together in mutual love and forbearance.

Now, my friends, you see that the HOLY GHOST is the Life of the Church. *Without* the HOLY GHOST the Church is a mere human society, a congregation of people who think much alike, and from which if they see things somewhat differently, they are at liberty to go forth. But *with* the HOLY GHOST, the Church is a living divine society, in which alone is life. Leave it; and you cut yourself from life, the HOLY GHOST ceases to influence and animate you; you are spiritually dead, like a foot or hand cut from the body.

Let me give you another illustration or two of my meaning.

You have seen a piece of machinery set in motion by

steam.   Here are wheels and there are wheels, fitting one to another by cogs, there are drums, as they are called, with great leather straps round them, which set other wheels in motion, and the whole when in action performs wonders. Go some morning early and look into the mill, there are all the wheels, and straps, and drums, and so on, in their places, doing nothing, just as they were turned out of the hands of the maker.   Presently a man comes and opens a little tap, and all at once, the whole springs into activity; the wheels revolve and set others in motion, the bands fly round and round on the drums, and make the carding or reeling or spinning jennies fulfil their appointed task.

The machinery as you saw it at first is like the Church before Christ gave the Holy Ghost; the machinery when the steam was turned on is like the Church after the Holy Ghost was given.

Look at your watches.   How delicate and intricate is the mechanism within; sometimes they tell the time, the hands go round and point out the hours and the minutes; but sometimes they stand still, and are quite useless.   The watch serves no purpose till it is wound up.

Now the Church before Christ gave it life, was like the watch unwound, the Church after the giving of the Holy Ghost is like the watch wound up and set a-going.

Now there are one or two little points in connexion with these illustrations that I wish to direct your attention to.

In the human body the life that animates it penetrates to every portion of the body, even to the hair and the nails.   In the machinery of the mill, or of the watch, all is in motion to the very smallest wheel.   In your watch some of the wheels move so slowly that they seem not to move at all, but they are revolving; they are participating in the motion of all

the mechanism, and, what is more, they are going at exactly
the rate necessary to make all go well.

So is it in the Church. The Life, the HOLY SPIRIT, animates every single member. None too poor, too base, too
young for the HOLY GHOST to be in and to move. The
little babe is brought to the font. It is a tiny wheel put
into the machinery of the great clock of the Church. Before the Sacrament it is only a little wheel. The moment
the sacramental words have been spoken, and the water
poured on its head, the little wheel is fitted into its proper
place, and the movement of the life of the whole catches
it, and carries it on in the great spiritual action of the
Church.

Now what is the work which the HOLY GHOST is doing
in the world? why is He moving in the Church, giving life
to all its members ?

The machinery of the mill is made for a purpose,—to
make cloth or yarn, or to grind corn.

The mechanism of the watch is made for a purpose,—to
tell the time of day.

What is the machinery of the Church made for? For
some purpose of course it is made, but for what purpose?—
YOUR SANCTIFICATION.

" We are bound," says S. Paul, " to give thanks alway to
GOD for you, brethren beloved of the LORD, because GOD
hath from the beginning chosen you to salvation through
the sanctification of the Spirit and belief of the truth : where-
unto He calleth you by our Gospel, to the obtaining of the
glory of our LORD JESUS CHRIST." (2 Thess. ii. 13, 14.)
And again, " This is the will of GOD, even your sanctification." (1 Thess. iv. 3.)

Sanctification means making Holy. The work of GOD the

HOLY GHOST in the Church is the sanctifying, or making holy and like CHRIST of every member of the Church; not by compulsion, understand,—there is no forcing men to be holy in the kingdom of GOD,—but the HOLY GHOST acts on the heart, surrounding it with every attractive influence to draw it to GOD. The HOLY GHOST also flows in the Church through the Sacraments to make people holy. The Sacraments are, so to speak, the springs whence holiness flows. When you are thirsty you go with a pitcher to the spring; so when you need holiness, you go to the Sacraments, and there receive it.

What stands in our way of being holy? First, our natural inclination to evil. Secondly, sin committed through yielding to this natural inclination to evil. Therefore we want help in two ways. First, help to overcome our natural inclination to evil; secondly, pardon for sin committed, so that we may not fall under the power of evil, and so our spiritual life come to a dead stop.

In the Sacraments you find help of both kinds,—strength and pardon.

So this is the work of GOD the HOLY GHOST in the Church, strengthening your weakness to overcome temptations to evil. Pardon for sin I shall speak of when I come to that article "The Forgiveness of Sins," it belongs less directly to the HOLY GHOST, than does strengthening.

You want your little children to grow up with divine grace to assist them to struggle against sin. Therefore you bring them to holy Baptism. Let them grow up without Baptism, and they grow up without any help from GOD, with merely their *natural* powers to protect them, and with a natural inclination very prone to evil. You take them to Baptism, and they are given *supernatural* powers,—the help of GOD, to assist them, and GOD'S grace to lead their wills to choose that which is good and abhor that which is evil.

So too when they are a little older, and are exposed to greater temptations. You know how the world and the flesh try to draw young people from the service of GOD, and obedience to His Commandments. Of course then they want more help. So they come to Confirmation ; in which Sacrament GOD the HOLY GHOST gives special strength to meet their new and special requirements.

So when people desire to be married. They are entering on a new state with new trials and new temptations. They want special help and grace for that state, to enable them to pass through those new trials and withstand those new temptations. They receive the blessing of the priest on their marriage, and with that receive from the HOLY GHOST what they require, that new grace adapted to their new requirements.

Then, again, when a man desires to become a minister in GOD'S Church, he needs special grace for the work, different in kind from what he needed before ; so he receives the Sacrament of Ordination, and therein the grace of GOD the HOLY GHOST is given him to enable him to administer Sacraments and to meet the temptations and trials of his new state, with GOD'S assistance, and not by his own power.

The will of GOD is your sanctification. He does not do all for you. As I said before, He will not force any man to be holy. He does all He can, and He expects you to do all you can. Grace is not given to make men lazy, but to brisk them up to work. And grace cannot sanctify or make holy, unless man *corresponds* to grace, as it is called, that is, unless he does all he is able to do to let Grace work out his Sanctification.

GOD sends the rain and the sun, but He expects you to till the fields and sow them so that sun and rain may perfect your work. Sun and rain will do no good to a farm when the farmer lies in bed and spends his working time in hunting, sporting, and fishing, and never ploughs, manures, sows, and cleans his fields. And a farmer may haste to rise up early and late take rest, ploughing, dressing, sowing, and cleaning his fields, but he will reap nothing, unless GOD sends sun and rain.

So is it exactly with ourselves. Our souls are our farms to be ploughed and dressed and sown and cleaned by us. Grace is the rain and sun to make them fruitful. All our labour without Grace is wasted. All Grace without our labour is powerless.

On the road to Colchester is a windmill. You know it: when the wind blows, the grindstone turns, the clapper goes, and the wheat is ground into flour. When the wind doesn't blow, no corn can be ground.

The wind won't grind corn without the windmill, and the windmill cannot grind the corn without the wind. The miller has provided all he can do and he looks to GOD to send him the wind. So with us. We must do what we can, and trust to GOD to help us when we can do nothing.

The theory of Grace is briefly comprehended in this saying: GOD helps those who help themselves.

XX.

THE HOLY CATHOLIC CHURCH.

" I speak concerning Christ and the Church."—Eph. v. 32.

I SPOKE to you last Sunday about the HOLY GHOST, the life and motion of the Church and all its members. Now I am going to speak to you about His Church itself. The piece of machinery, or the body, of which the HOLY GHOST is as the steam to the machinery, and as the soul to the body. You many of you belong to one or other club. You have a form, by which you are admitted into the club, enrolled among its members. I have seen gaily painted cards, framed and glazed in some of your cottages, with your name inscribed on them, to testify that you have become members of the Foresters', or the Provident, or the Odd Fellows' Club. As soon as you are members, you find that there are certain rules to be observed, and certain benefits to be obtained.

If I have not been enrolled in the Foresters' club, for instance, though I may keep all its rules, it is of no use my applying for the benefits. " You don't belong to the club," is the answer given me by the Secretary, so I have no right to receive the advantages it offers. " But," say I, " I have kept all its rules." " Very sorry," answers the Secretary, "but your name is not on the list of members."

And if I am enrolled, it is no use my applying for the benefits if I have not kept the rules. The rules are quite plain, I have them before my eyes, and I know the consequence if I disregard them.   By breaking the rules I forfeit my claims upon the advantages offered by the society.

That is all plain enough.   Now to apply it.

The Church is CHRIST's benefit club.   We are admitted into it by the form of Baptism.   By Baptism our names are entered in the list of members.   As soon as we are baptized we are bound by rules.   The rules are—to keep the Ten Commandments, and to believe the Creeds.   The benefits are—Grace here, and Heaven hereafter.

No use for one who is unbaptized to pretend that he has a right to the benefits.   He is not a member, he has no claims.

Nor has a member, who has neglected all the rules persistently any right to urge his claim on heaven.   He has forfeited it by breach of the law.

Now let us look at this in another light.

The Church is an army.

Soldiers are enrolled; that is they take their oaths of allegiance to the Queen, sign their names, and they are entered at once in the list of the servants of Her Majesty. From that moment they entail upon themselves certain duties.   They have to learn their drill, and when called upon, have to march to war, and fight against the enemies of their Queen and country.

But they are not called to fight with any such weapons and ammunition as they can provide for themselves.   On the contrary, they receive guns and swords, and are served out sufficient ammunition.   When they go to battle, the ammunition waggons follow, and they are furnished with as much gunpowder and shot as is necessary for them.   They get so much in peace, so much in war.

When the battle begins, they have to make the best use

they can of their weapons and ammunition against their enemies. They have promised to do this, and they are provided by Government with the requisite means.

When the war is over, the victorious soldiers are rewarded with a medal or a cross, or a pension.

Very well. The Church, I said, is an army. As soldiers are enrolled, so are churchmen. By baptism we are made soldiers of CHRIST. This is what the priest says when he christens a child, " We receive this child into the congregation of CHRIST'S flock, and do sign him with the sign of the cross, in token that hereafter he shall not be ashamed to confess the faith of CHRIST crucified, and manfully to fight under His banner, against sin, the world, and the devil ; and to continue CHRIST'S faithful soldier and servant unto his life's end."

As soon as the child is baptized, it has duties laid upon it, the duty to believe GOD'S truth, and to do GOD'S will. It is called to fight, but not in its own strength. It is served out with ammunition for the war. That ammunition is Grace.

Now a soldier in battle may, if he pleases, throw his cartridges away, or fire his gun into the air and desert. But, I will tell you what will be done to that fellow. He will be drummed out of the army, and shot.

So may we throw away all the grace given to us, wrapped up in sacramental cartridge cases. Or we may neglect to use it against the enemy of our souls. Or we may run away from the battle, and not fight at all.

What then ? The great court-martial at the last day will try us, and sentence us to degradation and death—death everlasting. Why ? because we have violated our promise when we became soldiers, and done despite to the Spirit of Grace.

But to those who are good soldiers and fight, there is a reward. When CHRIST our King comes to review His army at the general resurrection, He will reward His good and faithful servant with the crown of eternal life.

No use *then* for one of us soldiers to say, "I was enlisted in Thine army, LORD!" unless he fought when commanded. No use for one of us to say, "I received abundance of Thy grace," unless he made use of that grace.

No use either for a soldier to think he knows better than his officers, and go where he likes and fight with what arms he likes, and find ammunition for himself. Do you think a soldier would meet with much pity if, after the battle, his officer were to call him up, and some conversation like this were to ensue between them :—" Number 16, why were you not in your place in your regiment?" "Sir, I thought I could do better hiding behind a hedge at some little distance off, and taking aim where I could not be seen." "But I did not hear the report of your rifle." "Sir, I levelled my gun all the time, but it would not go off, as I had no gunpowder." "But why had you no gunpowder? It was served out at the regular time, and from the ammunition waggons." "Well, sir, I refused to take it, as I had a theory of my own that sawdust would answer as well; and I did not find out till too late that sawdust did not answer."

Now this is precisely what certain persons do. They will not occupy their position in the Church of GOD, and fight where GOD has called and placed them; but they go off after their own fancies, and level their guns anywhere but where they are required by GOD. One goes as a Bap_tist, one as an Independent, one as a Wesleyan, one as a Quaker, one as a Bible Christian, one as a Reformed Calvinist, anywhere but to his place in the army of CHRIST. And then, they reject the ammunition waggons of grace,— the Sacraments. They will have none of them. They have their own theories. So they try them instead of sacramental grace, only to find out when too late that *sawdust won't do*.

Next let me speak to you about who was the great founder of the Church.

One Robert Brown founded the Independents in 1585.

The Baptist sect was founded about the year 1521 by Carlstadt, Storck, Muncer and John of Leyden.

George Fox founded the sect of Quakers in 1646.

John Wesley was the founder of the Wesleyans in 1742, so that the Methodist sect is about 130 years old.

But JESUS CHRIST, Who is GOD, founded the Church nearly two thousand years ago.

Every sect changes its views as time passes. The old Baptists allowed men to marry as many wives as they liked, John of Leyden had seventeen.

Certain chapels were allotted to the Independents in England at the Restoration. Nearly all these chapels have become Unitarian. That is, the old Independent congregations have gradually become disbelievers in the Trinity, and in JESUS CHRIST as GOD.

John Wesley said, "If the Methodists leave the Church, GOD will leave them." Are they not separate and hostile to the Church now?

But the Church never changes, she has the same faith always and everywhere, for CHRIST promised that it should do so, " Lo I am with you always even unto the end of the world."

John Wesley, George Fox, John of Leyden, and Robert

Brown are dead and gone, and what can they do for their sects now?

Jesus Christ, the founder of the Church, lives and defends and sustains it, as its king, so long as the world lasts.

The founders of the sects were mere men, likely enough to make mistakes, to teach error. The founder of the Church, Jesus Christ, is God Almighty, the Truth itself, who cannot err.

The Church, in the next place, is the kingdom of Christ. In a kingdom there are laws, and officers to enforce those laws. In the Church there are laws, and officers. But there is this difference between the kingdom of Christ, and the kingdom of an earthly prince. If I break the laws of England, I am taken up by a policeman and am put into prison. If I break the laws of Christ's kingdom, I am not punished at once. The magistrates and officers of that kingdom do not punish, they are not sent to punish, but to teach us what the laws are, the punishment is reserved for Christ Himself to administer justly hereafter.

Then again, what makes a magistrate? He receives his commission to act as a justice of peace from the Lord Lieutenant of the County, who receives authority to appoint magistrates from the Queen. So in the kingdom of Christ. There are magistrates,—the priests and deacons. They are commissioned by the Lord-Lieutenants of Christ's kingdom,—the bishops, and the bishops receive authority from Christ, Who gave it to the Apostles to hand down from age to age to the end of the world.

But it is not so with the ministers of dissenting sects. They send themselves. They take their office on themselves. If one of you farm-men were to walk about the parish and attempt to take up any one who was driving too fast, he would snap his fingers in your face. He would say, Where is your authority? Who made you a policeman? So I say to dissenting ministers: Where is your authority? Who made you ministers? Show me your commission.

We have then, in conclusion, three great advantages in the Church of CHRIST.

We have the certain truth taught; there can be no doubt about it, for CHRIST is with His Church to protect it from falling into error.

We have officers or clergy, coming, not in their own name, or with their own authority, but in the name of CHRIST, and commissioned by Him to act with His authority.

We have the Sacraments, or means by which GOD gives us grace and strength and pardon. Without a ministry authorised by GOD to perform the Sacraments they can be only empty signs and bare forms, but with a ministry ordained by GOD, there is no such a thing as empty signs and bare forms, they are all filled to overflowing with divine grace.

And remember, my brethren, that as subjects of the kingdom of CHRIST, we are bound to observe its laws, and to observe these laws we need GOD's help, and GOD's help is given to us through the Sacraments, and we can only have Sacraments, if we have true bishops and priests commissioned by GOD, and we can only find such in the Church.

K

XXI.

THE COMMUNION OF SAINTS.

" Ye also helping together by prayer for us, that for the gift bestowed upon us by the means of many persons, thanks may be given by many on our behalf."—2 Cor. i. 11.

THE passage of the Creed, which I am going to speak to you about to-day, is one more neglected than any other by us members of the Church of England. Every article of the Creed is not only a truth to be firmly held, but it entails a practice growing out of the doctrine.

We believe in the Incarnation, therefore we build all our Christian worship, and lean all our prayers on the great truth that GOD the SON became Man. We believe in the sacrifice of the Death of CHRIST, therefore in the Holy Eucharist we plead that sacrifice with GOD the FATHER.

We believe in the HOLY GHOST, therefore we seek the grace of the HOLY GHOST through the Sacraments of Baptism, Confirmation, Ordination, &c.

We believe in the Holy Catholic Church, therefore we submit to its rule in faith and morals, and obey its ministers appointed by GOD.

We believe in the forgiveness of sins, and therefore we seek pardon through the precious Blood of CHRIST.

But when we say, we believe in the Communion of Saints, in nine cases out of ten, we do not know what we mean when we use the words, and in ninety-nine cases out of the hundred we have no practice corresponding to, and growing out of, the doctrine we profess to hold firmly.

The truths in the Creed are not dry husks of doctrine, but living realities, seeds from which an abundant crop of practice is expected to spring up.

Every truth in the Creed is like a different seed or root, and a perfect Christian practice should be like a flower-garden in which all grow up harmoniously. It does not do to let one have the upper hand, so as to displace other truths, or to leave out some. Let us call the Christian practice growing up out of the roots of doctrine proposed in the Creed by the names of different flowers, as roses, lilies, stocks, asters, chrysanthemums, dahlias, anemonies, geraniums, and so on. Now in a well ordered flower-garden these beautiful plants occupy their proper position, and bloom in their proper time. But what would a garden be like, planted only with red geranium? At one time of the year it would blaze scarlet, and vex the eye with excess of one colour. Or say with chrysanthemum. Then all spring and summer the garden would be bare of flowers, and we should have a show only in November.

Now we English Churchmen have neglected sadly the beautiful flowers of practice that grow out of the root, " I believe in the Communion of Saints." And this is the reason. Three hundred years ago, this practice had spread over the whole garden of Christian life, like a weed, strangling the other flowers, so that there was necessity for it to be cut back, and it was so cut back that it has not recovered itself since. But our garden looks bare without it. There is an ugly bald spot in our religious life for want of it; and it demands restoration, in proper moderation.

Now let us see what we mean by the doctrine of the Communion of Saints, and what are the practices which should grow out of it.

The word Communion is a Latin word which means exactly "a building or fortifying together." It means that there are two parties engaged on one common work, and that each has his share in getting it done. A bricklayer and his labourer are in communion, for one brings the bricks and mortar, and the other lays the bricks and spreads the mortar.

Now when we say that we believe in the Communion of Saints, we mean that we believe that the dead in CHRIST and we who are alive are working together for a common object, with mutual exchange of loving offices.

And what is the work on which they and we are engaged? On the advancement of CHRIST's kingdom, the making up of the number of the elect.

And how is that done? By the remission of sins and the perfecting of the faithful.

The popular idea of a good man when he is dead and buried is, "There's an end of him. I have nothing more to do with him, and he has nothing more to do with me." Now this is utterly wrong, and all arises from the fact that we have forgotten that we are called on to believe in the Communion of Saints. We have a great deal to do with him, and he has a great deal to do with us.

We can still pray for him, and he can still pray for us.

He wants our prayers, for he is not yet perfected. There is much of this earth still clogging his soul, and all this must be washed away before he can be made perfect; all his works, as the Apostle tells us, must be tried with fire. He must be gradually purified and made fit for the presence of GOD. When a man is dying, you will see in the Prayer Book, that the priest is instructed to pray that the soul on leaving the body may be cleansed and purged from the stains of evil "Wash it, we pray Thee, in the blood of that immaculate Lamb, that was slain to take away the sins of the world ; that whatsoever defilements it may have contracted in the midst of this miserable and naughty world, through the lusts of the flesh, or the wiles of Satan, being purged and done away, it may be presented pure and without spot before Thee."

So also the souls of the faithful departed pray for us. You are very much mistaken if you think that they have no more interest in us, that they do not think of you, feel for you and feel with you. And so we help on each side to build up, fortify, and strengthen one another.

But I dare say you are thinking, How can the souls of the faithful know about us and our thoughts and necessities ?

I think I can make you understand this, if you will give your attention for a moment. Some of you have got sons and daughters in America. Let me suppose that an old mother here who has a son in Canada wants some blankets for winter, it is getting daily colder, and the poor old creature shivers in her bed at night, and she thinks, "Ah ! if my John were only to know how cold and poor I am, he would send me a pound or two at once." So she writes to him a letter. The letter is taken to Colchester in the postman's cart, thence it is sent to London by train, where it is sorted out for Liverpool, and goes by the mail to Liverpool, there it is put in a bag for Canada and sent on board a steamship, which goes to America, and the bag is given out at Quebec, where it is sent on by boat and coach to the nearest post-office, and there it waits and waits till an opportunity arrives for it being sent to the back-wood farm. John is sore troubled, and he takes the first opportunity of getting a post-office order for a couple of pounds which he

sends off, and at last the old mother gets it. Well! she
wrote in October when the first frosts came on, and she
shivered all through November and December, and just
about Christmas gets the money and blankets.

There's a long affair about conveying intelligence of her
need to John, and getting back help from John! And why
all this time and trouble? Why simply because old Nanny
and John are both in the flesh; and being in the flesh are
dependent on material means for communicating with one
another.

But there is a simpler, and if I may use the term, more
spiritual mode of communication. That is the Electric
Telegraph, which sends its message flying to America in a
minute.

But the wires break, and then there is no more sending
messages till the cable is fished up and spliced again.

So there is something clumsy and material in that also,
yet we are obliged to use it, for being in the flesh, we must
use material means of communication.

But if we were in the spirit, it would not be so, a soul
does not want postal communication or telegraph wires, or
any material means for communicating with another soul.

Let us say that old Nanny's John had died in the back-
woods. Well, the moment old Nanny thought of her dear
boy, his soul would know it. No post-cart and train and
steamboat are needed to convey the news to him. And what
do you think the spirit of John would do? would he wish he
were back in the flesh that he might get a post-office order to
send to his mother? I think not. He would go direct to
GOD, the Father of the poor, and beseech Him to relieve the
necessities of the dear, shivering old mother. I know John
would do that: I know he would remember how his mother

sat up with him when he was a little child, rocking him to sleep in her arms, how she wrapped her own check-shawl round him when he was cold, and forgot herself, and I know that he would besiege GOD with prayer for his dear, dear, old mother, that she might receive comfort in her old age when left friendless and childless.

Some people fancy that death breaks all interchange of loving offices between relations and friends. That, for instance, a father may feel very anxious for the welfare of his children on Monday and be indifferent on the Tuesday, because he died on Monday night. That S. Stephen could pray for his murderers before the last stone smashed in his skull, and that the moment his spirit was free he could not pray for them. That supposing a soldier was cut down by a cannon ball whilst he was saying the LORD's Prayer, just at the moment he had got to "Give us this day our daily bread," the prayer would ascend to GOD in a broken bit, and that he would be unable to ask " Forgive us our trespasses."

I can only understand people thinking this on the supposition that they consider our bodies as praying machines, and that it is the body, not the soul, that prays ; consequently when the body is dead of course it can't pray. But if we hold that the spirit prays whilst we are in the body, then of course the spirit can pray when it is out of the body. The spirit does not require the piece of machinery called the body to pray with, so that it is utterly helpless when the machinery is broken.

Then, in like manner, some folk have got the notion into their heads that you may pray for a dying man when he is insensible, but the moment he is dead you can't properly pray for him any more. The nurse holds a feather to his lips, and as long as the feather flutters prayer is right, when the feather does not move it is wrong. You may pray for the soul whilst it is in the body, not when it is out of the body. This erroneous idea arises from the following mistake.

They think that man's state is irrevocably fixed the moment that the soul leaves the body. But there is not a text in Scripture to prove this. There is one often quoted, and that is, " If the tree fall towards the south, or toward the north ; in the place where the tree falleth, there will it be." (Eccl. xi. 3.) But Solomon is not talking about the condition of souls after death in this passage, but about something very different, as you may judge for yourselves, if you will turn up the passage in your Bibles.

Those who think souls are judged immediately on death forget that the Judgment is to take place at the end of the world. *Then* not *now.* And surely the dead need to have their sins remitted quite as much as do the living. They need to have their robes washed and made white in the Blood of the Lamb ; to be tried as silver is tried, and perfected so as to have all the dross of earth purged away, that they may be fit to enter into Glory at the last Day when the final sentence is given.

Now let me return again to what I was speaking about just now,—souls being able to feel for one another, knowing each other's wants instantly, and without difficulty.

You have seen the Northern Lights, or the Aurora, as it is sometimes called, how it throbs and flickers, and now and then sends up streams of white light. Well, my friends, it has been ascertained by scientific men, that when an Aurora is seen in England, an Aurora is going on everywhere about the world, it is going on in New Zealand, though the people there cannot see it, for it is day with them, when it is night with us.

Something more has been discovered. This is, that the second our Aurora throbs, at that same instant exactly the Aurora in New Zealand throbs, that the moment these magnetic lights shoot in Greenland they shoot in Terra del Fuego. Is not that wonderful! Well it may explain in some way how it is with spirits. When your souls throb with love to GOD, a throb of love goes through all the souls that are in Paradise. When you feel a good desire, it reflects itself in them. Instantly, by a spiritual impulse, obedient to a law, the law that governs souls. But we see it not. We are like the New Zealanders, who behold not the Aurora in their sun-illumined sky, and have no idea that above their heads a magnetic influence is answering a similar influence in Old England.

Now let me give you another resemblance. I was one night—it was a fifth of November—at some little distance from a place where a great bonfire was. It was cloudy overhead, and all I could see was a red reflection of the blaze in the sky. The clouds grew bright when the flame leaped up, and were dark when the fire went down. Presently, I suppose, some fireworks were let off, for the clouds overhead shone out and flickered white and blue and red and green and yellow in the most beautiful manner, repeating what was going on below.

Now that, I thought at the time, is an image of the great cloud of witnesses, the great heavenly host of saints and angels, looking down on and reflecting what goes on below, brightening when the Church grows bright, saddening when she is obscured with evil. And so do the holy ones who are with GOD reflect and sympathize with all the feelings of our souls, they feel for us in our struggles, sympathize with us in our sorrows, rejoice with us in our victories.

Now for the practical part of our lesson. I have shown you how closely we are united with the souls of the faithful departed. The practical application of our belief is twofold.

First :—Remember that whatever you think is visible to GOD, to the Saints and Angels and to all your relatives and friends who are gone to their rest. That they rejoice over your progress toward perfection, and that they pray for you when you fall.

Here is an encouragement in well-doing. Here is a reason for making efforts to keep the thoughts of the heart pure and right, to watch that they be not defiled with evil, obscured by selfish aims and worldly ambition.

And secondly :—Here is help in loneliness, in struggle against evil. You can call to your assistance all the host of the Redeemed to unite with you in prayer, to assist you in your fight. There are more that be with us, than they which be against us. We can concentrate the whole army of GOD on one point, the mighty host of heaven rushes to succour us when we cry out for help in the stress of battle, and are inclined to give way because we are alone.

Some say—This is putting many mediators in the place of CHRIST. What nonsense! When you are in trouble you ask your sister, or your mother, or your friend, or your priest to pray for you. Do you put them in the place of CHRIST? Is the Church interfering with CHRIST's mediatorial office every time the Litany is used, or the Prayer for all Conditions of Men?

Of course this practice may be abused, but abuse of a practice and exaggeration of a doctrine are not so bad as total neglect of a practice and disbelief in a doctrine.

XXII.

THE CONDITION OF FORGIVENESS.

" *The Blood of Jesus Christ cleanseth us from all sin.*"—1 S. John i. 7.

I TOLD you the other day that in the Church of CHRIST we were afforded certain privileges, that we obtain certain benefits which cannot be found outside the Church. I am going to speak to you of one of these to-day : the Forgiveness of Sins.

Before CHRIST came, men passed through life with the burden of their sins ever growing heavier, ever weighing them down more intolerably, unable to shake the burden off. They could not obtain pardon for their sins, because CHRIST had not as yet died to remit sins. The fountain for sin and uncleanness was not yet opened. All they could do was to wait, and look forward, and by their sacrifices show to GOD that they tarried, expecting the Lamb without spot who would nail their offences in His own Body to the tree. But now that CHRIST has come and shed His Blood for the remission of sin, we have only to seek pardon and we find it.

It is very necessary for you clearly to understand what the *conditions* are on which CHRIST forgives sin.

For you must understand that GOD acts towards us conditionally in everything. He gives us crops in due season *if* we till and manure our fields. He gives us health *if* we take reasonable care of our bodies. So He gives us forgiveness of sins with an *if*. What is the condition ? It is this : If we repent.

Now about Repentance. It is of the utmost importance

that we should understand exactly what true repentance consists of, so that we may qualify ourselves to receive forgiveness of sins. And please to remember, unless our sins are forgiven us, there is no admission into heaven.

So now the point to consider is, What is true Repentance?

True Repentance is made up of three parts, Contrition, Confession, and Satisfaction. In other words, and those easier to be understood, sorrow for sin, acknowledgment of sin, and resolution of amendment.

Next let me show you how these three parts necessarily make up true repentance.

One of you fathers has got a pear tree, and the tree yields a good crop, which you sell, and which goes some way towards paying your rent at Michaelmas. But you find out that your little boy has been in the habit of taking and eating the pears, and giving them away to his playfellows. You are angry, and justly so. Your little boy comes to you, and says, with tears streaming down his cheeks, and his voice broken with sobs: "Father, dear, I am so sorry, I have eaten your pears, but I never, never will steal them again." Then I think a loving father will forgive his boy. He sees that the boy is sorry, he hears him confess his fault, and promise amendment.

Now, would the father forgive the little lad if he did not think he was in earnest? if the boy only confessed and promised to be better in future, but showed no sorrow for what he had done? No; certainly not, for the father would have no assurance that the same trick would not be played again next autumn. There would be no *contrition*.

Nor would the father forgive him if he cried and promised not to take the pears, but would not acknowledge that he had taken them this time, but told a pack of lies about it.

No, I am sure the father would not forgive him. There would be no *confession*.

Nor would the father forgive the little boy if he cried and acknowledged his fault, but would not promise to try to keep his hands off the pears for the future, so that the father could only be sure that his son would not take the pears in the winter and spring, because there would be no pears then to take. No, I am sure he would not forgive him. There would be no *purpose of amendment.*

That is all very plain. You see that in dealing with your children you are ready to forgive them when they do wrong *if* they truly repent of the wrong done; that is, if they are sorry, confess, and resolve to amend. In our relations with GOD and sin it is the same. GOD is full of fatherly love, He longs to pardon His rebellious children, but He will not pardon unless there be true repentance, unless there be sorrow for sin, confession of sin, and an earnest purpose not to offend again.

It is of no use whatever your going down on your knees and saying, " We have erred and strayed from Thy ways like lost sheep. We have followed too much the devices and desires of our own hearts. We have offended against Thy holy laws. We have left undone those things which we ought to have done, and done those things which we ought not to have done." There is no use whatever, I repeat, in saying this, if we are not a bit sorry for having erred and strayed; for having followed the devices and desires of our own hearts; for having offended against GOD's holy laws; for having left undone those things which we ought to have done, and done those things which we ought not to have done. It is of no use whatever feeling a sort of effeminate sorrow for having done wrong, without a bit of manly resolution to keep out of the way of falling again. You know the sort of maudlin sorrow some of you feel after you have got drunk and spent far too much of your week's wages on drink on Saturday night. Sunday morning you are sorry about it; but you know as well as possible that next Saturday you will do just the same, and you do not even make a hearty resolve to keep out of the public house. That is not true repentance. GOD scorns such repentance as that, because it is a sham. He will have real repentance and not a make-believe.

There is a miserable heresy, that is, false teaching, common in England, which I must guard you against, as it cuts at the root of true repentance, and therefore stands in the way of forgiveness of sins.

This is the teaching, such as you hear in dissenting chapels, and read in little dissenting tracts. It is that Forgiveness is perfectly free and unconditioned; that we have nothing whatever to do but to accept a free pardon; that all our tears, and all our confessions, and all our earnest resolves are worthless. Pardon depends not at all on them, but is given perfectly independently of them by GOD.

We will bring this doctrine of "Justification by Faith alone," as it is called, to the touchstone of common sense, and see what it is worth.

Your little boy has stolen your pears. He believes in your goodnature, and because of his faith in your readiness to forgive, without requiring him to be sorry for what he has done, confess his fault, and purpose to be a better boy, you freely forgive him.

What is the necessary result? He says, "Father is so goodnatured, I have such a faith in his kindness and readiness to forgive, that I will rob his apple tree."

This you goodhumouredly pardon without there being any repentance in the child; so the boy says, "What a very goodnatured father, I can do anything so long as I believe. I will rob his nut tree." Again he is forgiven. He has only to say, "Oh, you are so good, father, I know you won't punish me," and you pass it over, because he has such a high opinion of you. Then he thinks, "How I can humbug father, he is so soft. I'll steal his watch." And still you smile and forgive, so then one fine day he breaks open your money-box and runs off with all your savings.

And what is the judgment of your neighbours? They all concur in saying, "It is the reward of your folly; serve you right."

What is the necessary result if you treat your son thus, and justify him for his faith only? Why, of course you make him worse.

Now do you think that GOD can possibly have sent His SON into the world, that JESUS CHRIST should have died on the Cross,—for the sake of making men worse?

But if this miserable doctrine be true, then infallibly the purpose of the Gospel was to make Christians worse and worse, the more Christian they became.

Suppose forgiveness is perfectly free, and you can have pardon for sin, if you merely believe and accept it; then why should you not become a thief, an adulterer, a liar, a murderer, to-morrow? It doesn't matter what you do, GOD forgives all sin, if only you believe. Away, away with such a doctrine of devils. I can only believe that it can have been invented and spread among men by the Evil One, that he might blind their eyes, and harden their hearts, that they might miss the only means of pardon which GOD has provided.

GOD's plan of forgiveness necessarily makes men better, raises them, and teaches them to honour Him, fear Him, and love Him; to honour and fear Him as a just Judge, to love Him as a tender Father.

But the Protestant plan leads to our moral ruin. It blinds us to GOD's justice. It makes all our religion consist in deceiving ourselves and trying to humbug GOD.

Next, as to the motive of Repentance. You may repent, either because you are afraid of GOD, or because you love GOD. It is easy to see which is the best motive, and which sort of repentance He most readily accepts.

Your little boy may be sorry for having stolen your pears, confess, and promise amendment, because he fears a whipping. And then you forgive him, but the terror of the whip is the only thing that you are sure will make him keep his hands off the pears in future.

Or, your little boy may be miserable in his heart, because he loves 'dear father' so much, and he knows 'dear father' will be dreadfully put out when he finds the pears gone, and so be short of money for rent day. Then the little fellow comes to you, throws his arms round your neck, hides his head in your breast, bursts into tears, and says, "Father, I am so sorry, I have stolen your pears, and I never will take them again."

Is not that the best, the most perfect sort of repentance?

Oh! how ready GOD is to forgive us if only we will show Him that our repentance is real, and that His readiness of forgiveness will be to us a source of strength and an occasion of improvement, and be not presumed upon by us so that it become to us instead an excuse for continuing in sin and falling under the power of Satan.

XXIII.

THE HOPE OF RESURRECTION.

"*As in Adam all die: even so in Christ shall all be made alive.*"—
1 Cor. xv. 22.

JESUS CHRIST did not come into this world, die, and rise again to do a half-work. He did not come *only* to save men's souls. He came to save men's souls and bodies.

If He had come only to save their souls, it would have sufficed if He had taken a human soul on Him without a human body, and suffered in soul only, not in body. But as He came to save the entire man, made up of body, mind, and soul, He took on Him, suffered in, and raised up again a body, a mind, and a soul, that He might be the bodily, mental, and spiritual regenerator of mankind.

Your bodies will rise again.

These very same bodies which are laid in the grave will rise out of the graves at the last day.

That is the key to the significance of our Burial Service. Why do we make so much of a body that will crumble into earth, and be a prey to worms? Why do we not throw it away, and shove it hastily and unceremoniously out of sight, like an old worn-out coat or gown, if it is only a clothing of the spirit, with which we have no more concern, in which we have no interest?

We lay the body reverently in the earth, with prayers and psalms and hymns, because that body will be raised again. We have not seen the last of that body. You who laid your old mother in the ground and heard the earth heaped over her, have not lost sight for ever of that dear face, with its kind eyes, and gentle smile. You who put poor baby under the grass sods the other day have not seen the last of the little pet. You will see your mother and your baby again. Not merely will your souls meet, but in body shall you see them, look into their bright eyes, clasp their dear hands, hear their loved voices again. Oh! just think of that meeting when you, in this green churchyard, see one another again. How you will clasp your mother in your arms. How when baby sees you it will give a cry, and rush to you.

What a wonderful morning that will be. All the white gravestones out there fallen, all the graves open, and the green turf thrown aside like a coverlet, when you spring out of bed; the stones in the church floor cracked, and the old dead priests and squires coming out at the door into the porch; that great mound on the roadside to Colchester scattered about, and a crowd of the old Danish warriors King Alfred buried under it, coming forth, strange and stern; the sea yonder foaming up on the beach, casting forth its dead, the drowned sailors standing on the sea wall looking up at the sky, and that sky all ablaze with light, angels flying here and there, their wings flashing, CHRIST enthroned on a white cloud, His feet on a rainbow, and Mary and the Apostles enthroned at His side, ready to judge the world.

It is perfectly certain that we shall rise from our graves in our bodies, the same bodies that died shall rise again. But though the bodies will be the *same*, yet they will be *different*. You have the same body that you had when you were a babe, but for all that it is different. It is the same body of the plant which is now the seed and then the flower, but for all that it is different. It is the same in essence, it is different in condition.

When CHRIST rose from the grave, it was the same body that died which rose again ; and as with Him so with us.

Now what will the difference be ?

The elect, those who have served GOD and are entitled to be called the children of the resurrection, will rise glorious. S. Paul says of the dead body, " It is sown in corruption ; it is raised in incorruption. It is sown in dishonour ; it is raised in glory. It is sown in weakness ; it is raised in power. It is sown a natural body ; it is raised a spiritual body."

You know a green caterpillar that ravages your vegetables in your gardens. It is generally found on the cabbages, and the cabbage leaves eaten into holes are due to that green insect. It is a nasty, fleshy, ugly creature. There is no beauty in it, it crawls sluggishly along, and spends its life in eating, eating, eating. It cannot rise from the cabbage leaf, it is a grovelling creature. At last winter comes, and then the caterpillar leaves off eating, and makes itself a little coffin, a glossy brown coffin, and it shuts itself up in this coffin, and lies quite still, as if dead, all winter. You may find heaps of these little coffins in your garden, your spade turns them up under the bushes, near their roots, and I dare say you are much puzzled to know what they are. They are, as I tell you, the dead caterpillars in their coffins. The winter passes, and the bright spring sun shines out, the violets are found in the hedges by the school-children, and the golden celandine stars the pastures, and in the soft May air you see white butterflies fluttering in the hedges, and dancing about your garden. Whence come these large white butterflies? Why, they have burst out of those brown coffins into which the caterpillars entered.

The white butterfly is the resurrection body of the green cabbage grub. It is the same, and yet it is so different, so different in its appearance, now so lovely, then so ugly; now so light and active, rising into the air, fluttering high in the sun, then chained to earth, crawling over a cabbage leaf, now scarcely eating, but living only for the joy of living; then living only to eat, and crawl. Here is a marvellous change. It is to us a figure of our resurrection. We can have no idea of the beauty and perfection of our risen bodies, and of the immeasurable difference between their condition and our present condition.

But we know this, that all that is imperfect in our present bodies will be done away then. We shall rise, not in old age, but in the bloom and beauty of youth. The wrinkles of care and the grey hair of age will have passed away. Those who in life have lost their limbs, will not rise halt or maimed, but with arms and legs. The blind will see, the deaf will hear, and the tongue of the dumb shall sing.

> "On the Resurrection morning
>   Soul and body meet again;
> No more sorrow, no more weeping,
>   No more pain.
>
> "Here awhile they must be parted,
>   And the flesh its sabbath keep,
> Waiting in a holy stillness
>   Fast asleep.
>
> "For a space the tired body
>   Lies with feet towards the dawn,
> Till there breaks the last, the brightest
>   Easter morn.

"But the soul in contemplation,
    Utters earnest prayers and strong,
  Bursting at the Resurrection
        Into song.

"Soul and body reunited
    Thenceforth nothing shall divide,
  Waking up in CHRIST's own likeness,
        Satisfied.

"Oh! the beauty, oh! the gladness,
    Of that Resurrection Day,
  Which shall not through endless ages
        Pass away!

"On that happy Easter morning
    All the graves their dead restore,
  Father, sister, child and mother,
        Meet once more.

"To that brightest of all meetings
    Bring us, JESUS CHRIST, at last,
  To Thy Cross through death and judgment
        Holding fast."

And lastly, there is a lesson for us in this great article of
our Creed, a lesson for us to take to heart, and one to make
us careful.

If these vile bodies of ours are to be raised again, if they
are to be admitted into the kingdom of the resurrection,
then must we keep them in reverence, in temperance, so-
berness, and in chastity. The body is holy. The body is
predestined to eternal life. To save these bodies of ours
JESUS CHRIST rose from the dead, therefore beware how you
sin against these bodies, defile those temples of the HOLY
GHOST which GOD has willed shall be built up again at the
last day. We shall be judged for sins of the soul and for

sins of the body. Certain sins affect and stain and scar the soul only; but sins of intemperance and unchastity affect and stain and blemish the body as well as the soul. "Flee fornification," says S. Paul, "every sin which a man doeth is without the body; but he that committeth fornication sinneth against his own body. What? know ye not that your body is the temple of the HOLY GHOST which is in you, which ye have of GOD, and ye are not your own? For ye are bought with a price: therefore glorify GOD in your body, and in your spirit, which are GOD'S." (1 Cor. vi. 18—20.)

XXIV.

ETERNAL FELICITY.

"Then shall the King say unto them on His right hand, Come, ye blessed of My Father, inherit the kingdom prepared for you from the foundation of the world."—S. Matth. xxv. 34.

WE have come now to the last article of the Creed, one that follows necessarily on the article in which we profess our belief in the Resurrection of the Dead.

We believe that we shall rise in our bodies, and that those bodies will be glorious. What is to become of them? Are we to lay them aside again? Is there to be a second death? By no means. We shall rise in our bodies, and live in these bodies for ever and ever. There is not a word in Scripture about our laying them aside again. CHRIST JESUS carried His risen body into heaven, and sat

down in it at the right hand of GOD, and in it will come
to judge the world. There is not a word in Scripture
about CHRIST ever casting off His body! No! throughout
eternity He will be the GOD-Man, the divine yet human
King of glorified human beings.

Now if we are to be hereafter in our bodies, we shall need
some place in which to be. So we read that there will be
new heavens and a new earth, wherein will dwell righteousness. This world will be consumed with fire, and its fashion
will change, but then after the fire the earth will rise again,
recreated to be the holy habitation of a holy people. It will
rise from its fire, which will purge out all that is foul, and
ugly, and evil in it, as we also from our fiery trial shall have
risen purged and purified, and it will rise glorious, glorious
as of old when GOD first saw all that He had made, and
pronounced it very good, glorious with the beauty earth
had before ever sin entered into the world, and saddened
and darkened the fair face of creation, and stained earth
with crime.

" The fire which consumes the earth," says an old writer,
" will not destroy it, but will purge it, as formerly it was
cleansed with water. So will heaven and earth pass away,
not in substance, but in form, not by destruction, but by
renovation of all things; for, we are told, the earth standeth
for ever. Only in the fashion which they now bear shall
heaven and earth pass away; in essence they shall subsist
eternally, as the new heavens and the new earth which the
saints of GOD shall possess, and in which their days shall
be long."

In like manner as the bodies of the just are identical
after the resurrection with those they have now, but different
in appearance because glorified, so will it be with the earth

and the heavenly bodies, they will be identical in substance, but different in condition.

"The world made for man," says an ancient father, "to a certain extent reflects man's condition. Man, had he not sinned, would not have died; so, perhaps, had he not fallen the world would not have been doomed to perish. Man sinned, and the earth has been constrained to serve him in his sin, and as the Apostle says, 'not willingly,' to bear the sins of mortal man, and to receive his body and become a partaker in his corruption. So when the number of the elect is accomplished, and all men die, the world will die too. But, in like manner as man will rise, and those chosen of CHRIST shall rise immortal and incorruptible, so shall the world also be delivered from the bondage of corruption, to be translated into the glorious liberty of the sons of GOD. And the world then, eternal, unchangeable, and glorious, will serve the eternal, unchangeable, and glorious sons of GOD."

But oh! how beautiful will be the new creation, surpassing all we can conceive. Here in England you have no idea of the loveliness in southern climes, of the richness of colour, the gorgeousness of flowers, their variety, their abundance, of the gay plumage of the birds, the loveliness of the insects. I remember one day in the South coming upon a tall flower, bright golden yellow, a tuft of blossoms, and this was covered with dazzling blue stars, blazing, sending out rays of light in the sun, just as if little bits of the blue sky had strewn themselves on the yellow flower, and these were shining with all their light as jewels. It was merely a number of wondrously beautiful little beetles clustered on the flower. But, oh! so exquisite was the sight, I remember—I was a little boy then—lifting up my hands and crying out with delight at the sight, and gratitude to GOD for having made anything so fair to glad my eyes.

And a well known naturalist has described how when he went to Jamaica and saw the flowers and the birds there, he felt his heart too full, he sat down and cried from excess of pleasure, the beauty was more than he could bear. Do you know how very lovely music sometimes brings tears into the eyes? So it is sometimes also with very lovely sights.

And this naturalist goes on to say, " I have gazed on some very lovely prospects, bathed perhaps in the last rays of the evening sun, till my soul seemed to struggle with a very peculiar undefinable sensation, as if longing for a power to enjoy, which I was conscious I did not possess, and which found relief only in tears. I have felt conscious that there were elements of enjoyment and admiration here, which went far beyond my capacity of enjoying and admiring ; and I have delighted to believe, that, by-and-by, when, in the kingdom of JESUS, in the dispensation of the fulness of time, the earth,—the *new* earth,—shall be endowed with a more than Paradisaical glory, there will be given to redeemed man a greatly increased power and capacity for drinking in, and enjoying the augmented loveliness. Doubtless the risen and glorified saints will have the senses of their spiritual bodies expanded in capacity beyond what we can now form the slightest conception of ; and as all then will be enjoyment of the most exquisite kind, and absolutely unalloyed by interruption or satiety,— the eye will at length be satisfied with seeing, and the ear be satisfied with hearing. I shall be satisfied when I wake up after Thy likeness, O LORD !"

Now for another point.

When we enter into life everlasting, all will not have equal glory. Some will be saints, others will be only saved. Some will be shining bright close to GOD, others will only have been plucked as brands from the burning. S. Paul tells us it will be like the stars, "one star differeth from another star in glory,—so is the resurrection of the dead." He, for instance, who has served GOD truly all the days of his life, will occupy a far higher place than will he who has only repented and turned to GOD on his deathbed. As we have served GOD, overcome sin, become CHRIST-like, so will our position be.

Would it be fair, think you, that he who has striven hard against his temptations, has battled victoriously through life, and goes into his grave chaste in body, having overcome all the allurements of passion, who has never given way to drunkenness, has been strictly honest in all his dealings, has sacrificed himself, his means, his time, his energies, to help others, whose whole life has been GOD-fearing and GOD-loving, should be no better off than some dissolute drunken sot who has brought shame and misery to his own family and to others as well, who is just converted at his last gasp?

Bring it to the test of common sense. How would such a doctrine work? Would it not be putting a premium on vice? Would it not encourage men to be bad, making it evident to them that they will be just as well off in heaven if they lead bad lives, give way to their lusts, injure the souls and bodies of others, as if they strove all life through at conquering their passions, and laboured to do good to the souls and bodies of others?

But there is one more point to consider.

Though our lots hereafter will be different in glory, some

shining bright as planets, others glimmering feebly as a tiny star,—yet the joy of all will be full. Each who enters into everlasting life will be perfectly happy. But the power of enjoyment will be much greater in some than in others. Cups may be of all sizes, and hold a quart, a pint, half a pint, or less. But all may be filled to overflowing. So will it be with all the redeemed hereafter. The joy of all will be full, though the joy of some will be much greater than the joy of others. The joy of each will be perfect, but the measure of perfection will be different to each.

From all this we learn a practical lesson. If our condition hereafter will depend on our lives here, as it infallibly will, how earnestly should we strive to resist sin and to advance in holiness. Every step forward, every victory over self and passion, every grace practised, places us a step higher and nearer to GOD hereafter, gives a brighter glory to our risen bodies, adds a jewel to our crown, expands our power of enjoyment, and satisfies it.

But every time we go back a step, give way to temptation, fall into sin, we are losing a place in heaven, we are giving up a higher and more glorious position for one lower and less bright.

Nothing that we do here for GOD can be lost. We shall be repaid hereafter in the way I have shown you, by obtaining a loftier stage of happiness, a position nearer to GOD. What an incentive to holiness! Every struggle against temptation gives you one additional joy hereafter. Every earnest practice of a Christian grace advances you a pace in proximity to GOD. The death-bed repentance is just the one stride which takes the man out of darkness into light; that is all. But a holy life consists of a constant advancing, a climbing of Jacob's ladder, a victory marking

each step. "Excelsior" is the Christian's cry, he cannot
rest, he must advance higher and higher, that he may
be perfect, even as his FATHER which is in heaven is
perfect, that the more abundant and brighter may he his
joy in the kingdom of the resurrection and the life everlasting.

J. MASTERS and SON, Printers, Albion Buildings, Bartholomew Close, E.C.